UNDERCOVER BABY

ADRIANNE LEE

HARLEQUIN®

TORONTO • NEW YORK • LONDON
AMSTERDAM • PARIS • SYDNEY • HAMBURG
STOCKHOLM • ATHENS • TOKYO • MILAN • MADRID
PRAGUE • WARSAW • BUDAPEST • AUCKLAND

ISBN 0-373-22609-8

UNDERCOVER BABY

Copyright © 2001 by Adrianne Lee Undsderfer

Visit us at www.eHarlequin.com

Printed in U.S.A.

ABOUT THE AUTHOR

When asked why she wanted to write romance fiction, Adrianne Lee replied, "I wanted to be Doris Day when I grew up. You know, singing my way through one wonderful romance after another. And I did. I fell in love with and married my high school sweetheart and became the mother of three beautiful daughters. Family and love are very important to me and I hope you enjoy the way I weave them through my stories."

Books by Adrianne Lee

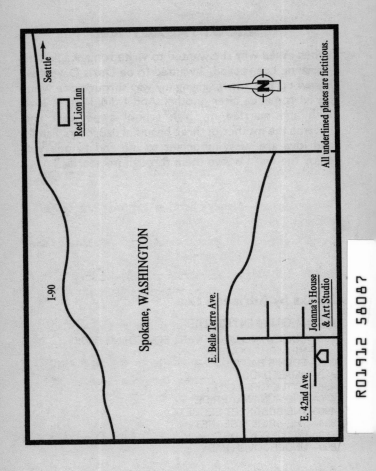

Seattle

I-90

Red Lion Inn

Spokane, WASHINGTON

E. Belle Terre Ave.

E. 42nd Ave.

Joanna's House & Art Studio

N

All underlined places are fictitious.

CAST OF CHARACTERS

Joanna Edwards—Seeking the daughter who was stolen from her, Joanna is brought face-to-face with dangers of the heart as well as the body.

Cade Maconahey—His baby has given this undercover vice cop the first sense of family he's ever had. He'll allow nothing and no one to take the child from him.

Nancy Wheeler—Cade's ex-wife is on the run and cannot be found.

Ted Wheeler—Nancy's brother is not telling all he knows.

Luna Cassili—Her past is as abstract as some of the art on display in her gallery.

Shane Addison—Womanizer and the leading candidate for governor, he aspires to keep his reputation "golden."

Kendall Addison—A patron of the arts, she is murderously ambitious.

Mel Reagan—Will do anything for the right payoff.

Bob Massey—He is furious that Joanna broke off their engagement. Is he after revenge or reconciliation?

For Brandi Kae, Savannah Lee and Laci Chantal.
You are my heart and my inspiration.

Special thanks to:
Anne Martin and Gayle Webster;
Robin McCurly, Seattle Police Officer;
and the Blue Whole Gallery, in Sequim.

Prologue

Holding the train of her formal bridal gown over her arm, Joanna Edwards paced the corridor of Spokane's Sacred Heart Hospital, but no matter how fast she walked she couldn't escape the fear engulfing her. What was taking so long? It seemed like hours since the ambulance had rushed her father here.

Stopping opposite the doors of the emergency room, she slumped against the wall. Her stomach ached and her hands trembled. The paramedics had told her the gunshot wound wasn't serious. Had they been wrong?

"Coffee?"

Joanna gave Luna Cassili, her best friend and maid of honor, a shake of the head. Luna's blond wig was cut short and anchored on one side with baby's breath. Her teal taffeta dress rustled with her every movement. Joanna glanced at the foam cup and felt her stomach heave. "I don't think I could keep it down."

Luna nodded, then turned to the lanky, brown-haired man at Joanna's side, who, in his black tie and tails, looked more like a high-school prom date than a thirty-year-old bridegroom. "Bob?"

"No thanks, Luna." Bob Massey's soft ebony eyes echoed Joanna's worry. "What's this town coming to?

Drive-by shootings in Spokane, of all places. I can't believe it.''

Joanna couldn't believe it either, but the only other explanation was unthinkable. No. She wouldn't even consider it. That was over, behind them, ended permanently six months and two weeks ago on the saddest day of her life. She moved closer to her fiancé, thanking God for Bob and his generous heart. She did love him—maybe not with the passion she'd once known, but with a comfortable, predictable kind of love.

She shoved aside a sudden sharp twinge of guilt. Bob had been there when she needed him most, had supported her, had seen her through the last horrible six and a half months, and before that even, and had loved her unflaggingly. Another man might have considered her actions tantamount to betrayal. Not Bob.

He was the kindest, most honest person she knew. He deserved someone better than she, someone who returned his love measure for measure. She'd told him this, but he still wanted her—even knowing she could never, would never again give her heart to any man...not completely.

Laying the palm of her left hand on his shirtfront, Joanna stared at her naked finger. By now she should have been wearing Bob's ring. She shuddered, remembering the speeding sedan, the startling flash of light, the burst of exploding glass as the back window of the limo blew inward, the bullet plunging through her father's arm, the liquid red blossom erupting on his gray tuxedo jacket. ''It's taking too long. I'm scared. Dad looked so pale. Maybe he lost too much blood. Went into shock.''

''Stop that.'' Bob pulled her gently against his chest

and rested his head on her beaded, chiffon hat. "He'll be fine."

Oh, God, please let Bob be right.

The doors to the emergency room swung open, sparking anxious shards through Joanna. She swiveled free of her fiancé's embrace and faced Dr. Park.

The elderly physician's concerned expression offered her little comfort. "Joanna, we've repaired the wound to your father's arm, but I'm afraid he's suffered a heart attack since being shot."

"No!" Joanna gasped. Her hands flew to her breast, over her own thundering heart. "How bad is he?"

"It was a massive coronary. He's stabilized, but very weak."

Bob caught her by the shoulders, holding her erect. "Is there anything that can be done?"

"He needs bypass surgery." Dr. Park glanced at one, then the other. "But at the moment, he's not strong enough to risk it. Maybe in another day or two…"

Joanna stared at him, numb, his awful pronouncement a possible death sentence for her father. This couldn't be happening. A pulse throbbed at her temple. "May I see him?"

"I want to move him to the Critical Care Unit. Get him settled first, but he's insisting on speaking to you *now*." Dr. Park narrowed his eyes, caution in every word he spoke, "Keep it short—and don't upset him."

On wobbly legs, Joanna made her way through the swinging doors to her father's bed. The tubes and machines attached to Lonnie Edwards reinforced the seriousness of his condition. His face was still unnaturally white, his lips blue.

Swallowing hard, Joanna blinked back tears and

took her father's hand, surprised at the coolness of it. "Hi there. You gave me quite a scare."

Lonnie's green eyes, so like her own, were strangely dull. He was only fifty-four, but looked at least ten years older. His thick black mane had gone completely gray in the past year, thanks to her. And now this. Guilt and fear twisted tighter than the knot at the base of her throat.

If only she hadn't met Shane Addison in Paris.

The wayward thought brought her up short. Would she continue to blame Shane for every bad thing that befell her and her family? Even her father's heart attack? Even knowing Lonnie was overweight, a sugar-loving, exercise-hating couch potato?

No. The police were certain it was a drive-by shooting. A random crime. No reason to suspect otherwise. Just a horrible incident that had led to even greater tragedy. Bad things happened to good people. And Lonnie Edwards was good people.

Maybe it was the wedding gift from Nancy Wheeler that had her thinking of Shane again. Receiving a gift from her had been strange. They hadn't seen Nancy in over six months. Hadn't even heard from her. Suddenly, out of the blue, she sends a wedding present. How had she known about the wedding? Had she kept tabs on Joanna all this time? If so, why?

Lonnie broke into her thoughts. "Please…forgive me."

The weakness of her father's voice set fresh worry bouncing around inside Joanna, making her more aware than ever that she mustn't let it show. "Don't be silly. The wedding will take place as soon as you're back on your feet." This assurance seemed to aggravate Lonnie more, but Joanna shushed him. "No, don't talk. Rest—or I'll go."

To her relief, Lonnie closed his eyes and seemed to sleep.

But he looked suddenly so frail, robbed of his usual indestructible mantle, like a felled knight of the Round Table. A band of fear wrapped around her heart. He was all the immediate family she had. *Dear God, don't let me lose him.*

As though he'd heard her thought, Lonnie opened his eyes again. Sweat beaded his forehead. "Say... you...forgive...me."

Apprehension twisted inside her. She could see his agitation increasing, his complexion graying. Tears burned the back of her eyes. Maybe she should get the doctor. "Dad, hush. I don't have anything to forgive you for and if you don't relax, I'll have to leave."

Lonnie lay quietly for several seconds, pain etched in the taut lines of his mouth, then his guilt-ridden gaze again sought Joanna. "Not...drive...by."

Joanna stiffened. "What?"

"Shane..."

"No," she denied. "He doesn't need to worry about us anymore."

"Shane..." her father repeated.

Joanna's pulse faltered. *Shane*. His image flashed into her mind. His white-blond hair, brown-lashed hazel eyes, the bump on his nose, his quick grin—that she'd since learned was practiced, phony—all brought home to her in a rush of bitter reminiscence, resurrecting a wealth of regret, revulsion, and, yes, fear. "Why would Shane send someone after us now? We aren't a threat to him any longer."

The heart rate monitor's display beam jumped erratically as Lonnie said on a raspy breath, "The baby."

Joanna felt as if the floor had turned to water beneath her feet. *Her baby.* She had loved her from the instant she'd known she was pregnant. The wound of losing her was still too fresh. Biting back a sob, she swallowed hard. Her daughter's precious life had ended before it began. Joanna hadn't even seen her. Had been too ill and had passed out. By the time she'd recovered, it was too late. All over. The baby was in the hands of the mortician.

"Don't bring this up now, Dad." Gripping the side of the bed to steady herself, Joanna leaned closer, closed her eyes and released a lung-bursting breath. "It's over. Done. Shane no longer has any reason to fear us or to hurt us."

"Does! Must have discovered—" The mechanical bleeps skittered.

Joanna stiffened in alarm. Her palms were damp, her hands unsteady, belying her strength to deal with both her painful past and her awful present. "Please, Dad, don't—"

"Must!" Anguish contorted her father's features. He drew a hollow wheezing breath. "Not...over."

Chilly fingers clutched Joanna's heart. The warmth dropped from her cheeks and she knew her face was as white as her wedding gown. Her gaze locked with Lonnie's. "Why do you keep insisting it's not over?"

"Baby," Lonnie murmured in an eerie croak, "not...stillborn."

"Not stillborn?" Blood thundered in Joanna's ears, cutting off all other sound. She couldn't breathe. For a long moment shock paralyzed her limbs. Confusion controlled her thoughts. "What are you saying?

Whose ashes did we bury? Where is Maddy? My Maddy?"

Lonnie's features twisted with pain and his eyes glazed. "God...forgive me." He gasped and went limp, then motionless.

"Forgive you?" The significance of his confession struck Joanna full force. Disbelieving horror tore through her, ripped open old wounds and constricted the muscles in her throat, reducing her voice to a strangled whisper. "What did you do with my baby?"

Her father didn't answer. His glassy eyes just stared at the ceiling.

"Dad!" Conscious of neither the machine's flattened ribbon nor the steady bleat of the alarm, nor the sound of rapidly approaching footsteps, Joanna screamed again and again, "Where is my little girl?"

Chapter One

"I swear if I find her, I'll kill her." Cade Maconahey clutched the phone between his jaw and ear, and gently bounced the noisy baby on his lap. Anger for himself, but mostly for this innocent child, fueled his temper. "She's pulled a lot of fur-balled schemes in her time, but this takes the prize."

"I haven't spoken with her in at least ten months, myself," said Ted Wheeler, Cade's ex-brother-in-law, a lawyer with a prestigious firm in Redmond.

"None of her old friends have either," Cade said.

"Midwifery keeps her on the move. She goes where the work is," Ted said. "Guess what we need is her day planner."

"Unfortunately, that wasn't among the things your wacky sister left on my doorstep." Cade's frustration echoed through the phone line.

He heard his former brother-in-law chuckle. "Precisely why your marriage never worked. She's lovable but kooky."

"What she is, is undependable."

"Unpredictable." Ted agreed.

"Irresponsible."

"Irritating."

"Infuriating." Cade ground out the word. But as he thought about the woman he'd once married, his anger lost some of its bite. Just how had he landed in this predicament? Self-disgust flushed his tense muscles. He knew precisely how part of it had befallen him. Divorced for five years, Nancy and he would occasionally get together for dinner, an evening of cocktails and chat, and often the night would end with their making love, as it had on *that night* fifteen months ago. They'd used protection—he gazed down at the baby—which had, unarguably, failed.

God, he never should have slept with her. How many times had he berated himself this week for that already? The problem was, the affection between them remained, an undying sexual spark that, when their guards where down—from too much wine—sometimes got the better of both of them. But even then, there wasn't enough attraction for him to ever make the mistake of thinking he could live with her again. Of course, at this moment, he'd be willing to give that a try—for the sake of their six-month-old son. "How could she do this to me?"

"To *you?*" This time Ted's laugh was derisive. "Might I remind you, my friend, that it takes two to tango? That child didn't come about by Immaculate Conception."

Cade clenched his jaw, keeping in an angry retort, knowing he was as ticked off at himself as he was with Nan. Why hadn't she told him? Before the baby was born? Or in all of the time since he was born? Why had she dropped him off and run away?

Ted broke into his dark thoughts. "So, are you adjusting to fatherhood yet?"

Cade swore beneath his breath and glanced down at

his son, feeling a mixture of protectiveness, posses-
siveness and overwhelming fear. A week ago he'd
been in shock. Today he was in love—with this child
he'd never even suspected existed. He was so small,
dwarfed by Cade's huge arms, a toy-sized human
whose very well-being rested in Cade's large clumsy
hands.

The baby had the phone cord caught in his dimpled
fingers, tugging it toward his mouth. He sure seemed
to drool a lot. Was that normal? "I can't do this alone.
I don't know anything about babies."

"Well, if that's Cody cooing in the background, I'd
say you're not doing too badly. He's still alive."

"Just barely." Cade almost laughed. Nancy had left
him formula and diapers enough for a couple of days,
along with instructions on how much and how often
Cody would be in need of both. For a thirty-year-old
cop who'd won the respect of his fellow officers for
fast thinking and keeping a cool head in a crisis, Cade
had suffered his first and worst defeat at the hands of
an infant.

A regular fumble-fingers. He couldn't seem to stop
tearing off the adhesive tabs on the diapers, not to
mention getting the diaper in place before his son let
loose and sprayed him in the face or down his shirtfront. Between pee and puke, he smelled like something left in a First Avenue gutter.

Actually he was glad no one on the force could see
him now. His house looked like a street gang had ran-
sacked it. Baby-food graffiti covered the kitchen counters, walls and floor. His and Cody's clothes hung
from living-room chairs and lamps. He needed a
shave, a shower, a change of clothes. Again.

Only the baby looked decent. *He* was fed and dry.

For the moment. He even smelled of a sweet, warm, milky scent that Cade thought he might never tire of smelling. However, used to order and calm, he felt himself losing his grip. He couldn't manage this full-time alone. He needed help. Cody needed his mother. Cade needed her, too. "It's been a week. I took a leave of absence from work. I can't stay out indefinitely."

"Did you know Nan still has her apartment in Issaquah?"

"No. Last I spoke to her she was in Spokane. Has she been staying at the apartment?"

"Nope. Landlady hasn't heard from or seen her in months. Ditto her neighbors."

"That's odd. Why keep the apartment if she isn't going to return to it?" Cade asked more to himself than Ted. He shifted the baby on his lap and felt a telltale wet spot on the leg of his sweatpants. He groaned inwardly, aware of the washer and dryer humming in the background; he wouldn't have a change of clothes until this newest load was done. "Did you ask where the rent checks have been coming from?"

"She paid a year in advance, before she left last time. Her lease is up at the end of this month."

Cade wondered again why Nancy had left the baby and run off without word about where she was going and why. If it was a job, she would have no reason not to tell him. But given the fact that Nan was neither a normal nor levelheaded woman... He silently cursed. If she were normal and levelheaded, he'd be worried as hell about her. But she'd proven too many times in the past how irresponsible she could be.

He lifted the baby to his shoulder. Cody grabbed for Cade's dark brown hair that had spilled across his forehead, caught a handful in his vise grip and tugged.

Wincing, Cade grappled with the phone and freed himself, but the pain in his scalp lingered. "We've got to find her. Soon."

"Too bad you're an only child. Got any aunts or cousins in the area?"

"No." *An only child?* Something hot and uncomfortable heated every muscle in Cade's body. He hadn't been an only child; he'd been an orphan. Turned over to the State the day he was born. He'd never known any of his family. Never felt driven or compelled to find the people who'd abandoned him to his own devices. The hell with them. But he wouldn't wish his upbringing on any kid. "No family."

"If Mom was still..." Ted's voice trailed off. Mrs. Wheeler, Nancy and Ted's mother, lived in a nursing home near Nan's apartment in Issaquah. She had advanced Alzheimer's disease.

"Yeah, well, that's not an option." He jostled phone and baby. The baby spit up, and a gush of warm white liquid spilled down Cade's T-shirt. Cade flinched, then groaned softly.

"Don't tell me you don't have any lady friends who'd be willing to help you through this crisis? Surely a handsome police detective hasn't got problems meeting women?"

Handsome? Cade caught his reflection in the toaster, his dark brown hair stood on end, his strong jaw looked black with whiskers, dark patches underscored his blue eyes. He was as handsome as a junkyard dog. He called Ted a name.

Ted laughed. "Women friends. Surely you have some?"

But that was just it, he didn't. None he'd trust with his son. Cade was a workaholic, an undercover vice cop. His job left him little time for a social life. He had to admit, since the divorce, he'd liked it that way. He'd been a loner from childhood on. Maybe he wasn't any more capable of maintaining a relationship than Nancy was. "Women I encounter through work fall into two categories—suspects or witnesses."

"Not a great dating pool, I guess."

"Not to mention that dating any of them would present a conflict of interest."

"What about a local agency? An au pair or nanny?"

Icy cold filled his belly at the thought of putting his son into the hands of a stranger, the way he'd been more often than he cared to remember from as far back as he could recall. He wouldn't do that to this little boy. *His little boy.* "That's not an option."

"Okay." Ted clearly didn't understand. "Then you're back to the women friends."

"Even if I did have a slew of women friends, I wouldn't want to push more strangers on this little guy. He cried a lot the first couple of days. I think he's been shuffled around too much in his young life, seen too many strange places and stranger faces."

"Yeah, probably. So, when was the last time you saw my sis?" Ted asked.

"You mean before last week when she dumped this in my lap?"

"Yes. Wherever she was might give us some place to start looking."

Cade stood and stretched his six-four frame.

"Fifteen months—but I spoke to her about nine months ago."

"And she didn't tell you she was pregnant?"

"That wasn't why she called." She'd called with some fantastic story about the leading gubernatorial

candidate being involved in the attempt to murder a
friend of hers in Spokane. He'd been sympathetic, but
Spokane was out of his jurisdiction. Besides, even if
he'd been inclined to investigate her charges on his
own time, she'd had no actual proof that Shane Addison had tried to kill her friend. It sounded to Cade
like another of Nan's far-fetched stories. "She needed
some help for a friend."

"Well, maybe that friend can give us an idea where
to find her."

"No. That's a dead end."

"Oh, you called the friend, then."

"No." Cade mentally kicked himself again. "Nan
didn't give me her friend's name."

WITHOUT A NAME, Joanna couldn't get a birth certificate from the state of Washington's Department of
Vital Statistics. Every newborn was registered by
name. She didn't know what name her daughter had
been given. Certainly not the one she'd wanted her to
have. Not Madeleine Rose Edwards. Joanna felt numb.
Two weeks' worth of numb.

She'd buried her father amid a mixture of shock,
horror and outrage. How could he have stolen her
baby? Allowed her to think her baby girl had been
stillborn? Her father, the one person she'd always been
able to count on in her life, was no longer there to
ask. To explain. To tell her where her daughter was.
Her rage was quickly spent in grief and desperation.

She glanced around the house she'd shared with her
father, for all of her twenty-six years the only home
she had ever had. Bars still covered the windows, safe-
guards added this past year against the constant threat
of unexpected attackers sent by Shane Addison.

This September morning had started warm, humid, and the occasional wayward breeze stealing through the open windows was welcomed. If only the task ahead were as welcomed. As threat-free. Reminding herself that she mustn't allow desperation to make her incautious, she dropped her bathrobe into the half-filled nylon suitcase awash in the sea of clothing on her double bed.

"I don't understand, Joanna, why you won't let me help." Tension lifted off Bob Massey like steam from a boiling kettle. He glared at the suitcase, then at her, obviously thinking she'd lost her mind, or at least her grasp on reason. "It could take months or longer to find the baby. Why can't we just get married and then go and look for her together?"

Joanna stopped packing. She released a heavy sigh, feeling the world pressing in on her, its weight too much to bear. In the last two weeks, the veil had lifted from her terror-constricted mind and she'd finally faced the mess she'd made of her life, was continuing to make of her life. She'd been a prisoner in her own home, rendered incapable of arriving at rational decisions and choices. She was partly responsible for her father's death.

She was wholly responsible for the predicament with Bob, and only she could fix what was wrong with this real-life portrait. If only the rectification could be made by simply picking up her brushes and palette. She feared she was about to hurt Bob in ways that might never mend. She took a deep breath, releasing it slowly. "Bob, I don't want to—"

"Then don't," he interrupted, stepping closer to her. "Just don't say it."

She frowned, her gaze meeting his, the pleading

look in his ebony eyes enough to break her already fragile heart. She and Bob had known one another since second grade when the Massey family bought the house next door, where Bob still lived. They'd been childhood friends. Teenage buddies. Shared a love of jazz and rock climbing and could finish each other's sentences.

But until the past nine months there had been nothing romantic between them, should never have been anything romantic. She closed her eyes, realizing she was about to lose her dearest male friend. But it was the first step in regaining control of her life. "I can't marry you."

His forehead creased with disbelief. "But why? I love you. You love me."

"Yes, I do, but as a sister loves a brother, not in the way you deserve and need. I can't marry you. It wouldn't be fair."

"We've had this conversation. I told you I don't care if you don't love me as much as I love you. That will come…eventually."

"No, Bob. We were fooling ourselves to think it would."

His face reddened. "I was there for you when you were pregnant with another man's child, there for you through the attempts on Lonnie's and your lives, held you when you wept for the loss of your baby, buried her ashes with you."

Joanna's throat constricted with guilt. "But don't you see? I was a sponge soaking up your generosity, your kindness, your love. Taking advantage of you out of sheer need. I didn't realize it until after Dad's funeral. Didn't want to face what I was doing or look at the consequences, and now Dad is dead because of that. And you're in emotional ruin. All my fault. I'm not giving you excuses. Just stating the facts. I needed someone to help absorb the pain and you were there. Thank God you were there. But I can't marry you for all the wrong reasons.''

She let this sink in for a few minutes, then added, ''I hope one day you can forgive me.''

''Forgive you?'' He looked as though she'd slammed into him with her car—physically buckling over, soul-deep hurt in his gaze, in his expression, a big, burly wounded puppy. Tears filled his eyes.

And hers. She hated herself for doing this. But wasn't it better to cut the cord swiftly and cleanly? Wouldn't dragging it out only hurt him worse? She picked up the engagement ring he'd given her from her nightstand and offered it to him.

He stared at it, but didn't reach for it. She caught his hand in both of hers, put the ring into his palm and curled his fingers over it. ''Please. You know this is the right thing.''

His eyes reminded her of a storm-riddled sunset, flashes of brilliant red light poking through dense black clouds. She pulled away from him, stepped away, but the need to explain still gripped her. ''I have to end what Shane Addison started or die trying. It's not your fight, Bob. It was never your fight. And I can't continue putting anyone else I care about in danger.''

He scowled, air blowing from him like a gust of wind. Fury punctuated his words. ''I'd be putting myself in danger.''

''No. I won't let you.'' Heat rushed into her cheeks. She would not budge on this point. This was her war. Only hers. ''I've lost my father and my daughter all because I allowed a man to make a fool of me. I need to end this. It's between him and me.''

"Between you and him—'' He choked on the word, then clamped his lips together as though slamming a door. His ensuing silence was like a scream. He shook his head hard, as though shaking off all trace of her, like turpentine on an oil painting washing through the colors, blurring them, erasing them. He moved away from her, plunged the hand holding the ring into his pocket and stalked from the room.

The walls seemed to vibrate, thrumming with the echo of his pain, her guilt. Joanna hugged herself, sucking in the tears that burned her eyes. She stood there a long moment staring at the empty doorway. In a moment she heard someone coming down the hall. Was Bob returning?

Luna Cassili, wearing peach silk capri pants, a gold silk shell and high-heeled sandals, earrings that hung to her shoulders and sparkled with every movement of her head, came into the room holding two steaming mugs.

She'd spent the night, but Joanna hadn't realized she was awake. The aroma of coffee filled the air. She set Joanna's mug on the nightstand. Today's wig was a black, chin-length number that brought to mind Cleopatra movies of the fifties. "I passed Bob in the hall. He looks like he's lost his best friend.''

Joanna turned back to her packing, folding underwear into the suitcase. "I told him.''

Luna nodded and took a sip from her mug. Luna and Joanna had been friends since they were thirteen. She had started life as Lucia Cassili, but everyone called her Lucy. She'd suffered most of her childhood with *I Love Lucy* and Lucy from *Peanuts* jokes and references.

During the summer of her thirteenth year, all of that changed. She'd become pregnant. Her parents made her give up the baby for adoption. She'd been so traumatized by the whole experience she'd lost all of her hair. Alopecia, the doctors said.

For most girls starting through their teens, these events would have been devastating. But not for Lucy. She refused to discuss the pregnancy or the baby, even to this day. As to her hair, she'd declared that since she was as bald as the moon, she would embrace its essence. From that day on her name was Luna. From that day on, she had also embraced the flamboyant side of her nature.

As Joanna's grandmother was fond of declaring, "She was no bigger than a minute." Petite she was, but Luna never entered a room without turning heads. Such was the power of her personality.

Joanna had respected her from that day forward. They'd remained fast friends, and now had a business relationship, as well. Luna owned Galleria de Cassili in downtown Seattle and was actively trying to sell two of Joanna's watercolors. If either sold, it would be the first profit from her art.

Today, *that* seemed so unimportant.

Luna looked her over now with her discerning eye. "Promise me you'll eat. You've lost so much weight you're swimming in that sundress."

Joanna swung toward the mirror over her dresser, swiping strands of her jaw-length, taffy-blond hair from her heat-sticky cheek. Two weeks ago, this white, crinkled-cotton sundress—extracted from her trousseau for the honeymoon that would never happen—fit perfectly. Now it fell from her shoulders like a painter's smock, the gathered waistline hovering near her hipbones.

She plucked a wide teal belt from the jumble of clothing on the bed and tied it like a sash around her middle, then bloused the excess fabric over it. Luna nodded in approval. "Well, that hides the problem, but it's no fix."

Joanna sighed. "You can't force-feed an unwilling stomach, you know."

Luna moved to Joanna, lifted a hand to her shoulder and squeezed gently, sympathetically. "You're going to find her, Jo."

"God, I pray you're right." Joanna wondered if Luna ever thought of the child she'd given away. Ever harbored any yearnings to find him or her, to reclaim him or her now that she was grown and self-sufficient. She had never broached the subject, nor would she, but it comforted Joanna to know that her friend understood how she felt. That was more than she could say for Bob. She returned to her packing. "If I can just find Nancy Wheeler."

"No luck there, huh?"

"Nope." Joanna pressed her lips together. Her cousin, Kenner, a computer genius in her estimation, had found Nancy Wheeler's ex-husband, Cade Maconahey, on the Internet the night before, but no information at all on Nancy Wheeler.

Luna sighed. "It's like she's disappeared off the face of the earth."

Joanna blanched. Hearing her greatest fear spoken aloud turned her stomach. She grappled the worry aside. If she gave in to it, she'd be lost before she'd begun. The trouble was, if Nancy had been a legiti mate midwife, she'd never have suited her father's purposes. The fact that Nancy operated just south of the law made locating her by the usual means impossible. Joanna could only hope that Cade Maconahey didn't share his ex-wife's love of deception and deceit. She would not, however, dismiss that possibility before meeting him. "If her ex doesn't know where she is, maybe he'll have some idea of how to find her."

Wiping a trail of moisture from the side of her face, Joanna crammed her slippers into the suitcase, zipped it and lowered it to the floor. She draped a teal-and-white jacket over her arm, then gripped the suitcase handle, placed her purse under her arm and left the house.

The two women stepped into the bright sunlight and walked to an old blue Mustang parked in the street. The neighborhood, Joanna noted absently, was unusually deserted for seven o'clock on a Monday morning. No sign of anyone, not even Bob. Yet, her nape prickled.

She checked the street in both directions, alert for any unknown or unfamiliar vehicles. She spotted none. She moved to her car, giving it a thorough once-over, looking for signs that someone had left her a nasty present, like a bomb. Since her dad's murder, she'd gotten even more cautious, even more jumpy. She found nothing to explain the uneasy tension rippling her nerves. She deactivated the car alarm and unlocked the trunk.

All night the temperature had hovered in the high sixties and now felt as if it was speeding through the seventies. Luna said, "After five or six hours of driving in this heat you'll be wilted by the time you reach Auburn."

Joanna gave no thought to the heat. She set her suitcase into the trunk beside the spare tire. "I'm going straight to his home. I'll phone you if and when I have something to report."

She slammed the trunk lid harder than necessary, disturbing the quietude and punctuating the turmoil in her soul. *Cade Maconahey, please have information for me.*

Luna hugged Joanna, stepped back, allowing her to get into the car and start the engine, then leaned in the window she'd lowered. "FYI. Just in case, I stuck a granola bar into your purse."

"Thank you." Joanna gripped her friend's tiny hand. "I'm worried about Bob. I've really hurt him and I—" She broke off, uncertain what she expected Luna to say or do about Bob. She supposed he'd have to work through this, the same as she.

"You've got enough to worry about keeping yourself safe."

"I know." Joanna shuddered. She had to stay alive, find her daughter and bring down Shane Addison. She wished that thought didn't fill her with foreboding.

"I wish I hadn't made appointments now with those two local artists. I ought to be driving with you this morning, playing shotgun," Luna said.

"That would have been nice, but you didn't know what I'd planned when you came over last night. I'm just glad you showed up. I couldn't have gotten through this morning without you." Joanna joggled her rearview mirror until it met her approval, again inspecting the street behind for any suspicious-looking cars, terrified that someone might follow her, and attempt to run her off the road, or shoot her as they had Dad.

Luna broke into her thoughts. "What will you do if this Maconahey guy can't or won't help you?"

Joanna silently shook herself. "Since he's a cop, I'm betting he'll want to keep Nancy out of jail. Because if he won't help, I swear I'll press kidnapping charges against her."

Chapter Two

Fear and anxiety rode with Joanna on the six-hour drive to Auburn, Washington. She kept watch for potential murderers; every mile made her nerves as taut as stretched canvas. She worried about whether or not Cade Maconahey would be willing and able to help her; every thought on the subject gave her unsettled stomach another brush stroke of misery and pain.

And beneath it all was the niggling concern about Bob. How she wished things had been different, had developed differently, that their friendship hadn't moved into the realm of romance. If she had been herself these last months, she'd have seen that, taken better care not to allow it. Now she'd lost not only a fiancé, but a dear friend, as well. Damn it to hell anyway. And damn Shane Addison.

She reached Auburn exhausted, yet oddly exhilarated, running on hope and expectation. As she slowed for the off-ramp, she thought how this once-fertile valley had been the home of local dairy farmers, the fields alive with cattle and crops. Too soon, growing industrial enterprises had taken over, the rich dirt covered with concrete, the lush green fields paved with progress.

Now the town, growing yearly by leaps and bounds, sprawled in both directions on either side of Highway 18. She turned left, merging into the busy traffic moving along Auburn Way North, the road leading into and out of the town's main business section.

Joanna listened absently to a local radio station's hourly newscast, catching only the last few words, "At ten before one on this glorious Monday, the temperature is eighty-eight degrees and rising."

Three blocks along, she took another left. Maconahey's house was near the library and an adjacent park, on a quiet street lined with oak and elm trees. His was the third house from the end, a redbrick rambler with a basement, circa 1950 or 60.

Her heart hitched as she pulled to the curb and shut off the engine. The sudden stillness of the car filled the interior with warm oppressive air, and Joanna felt as if she were being slowly smothered.

With her gaze riveted on Maconahey's house, she slipped from the car. The front yard was postage-size, the flower beds symmetrical and well tended, as though whoever lived here knew and enjoyed the care of plants, and loved roses in particular.

She strode along the sidewalk to the front door that was painted white and looked crisp against the red of the brick. She rang the bell, heard it echo within, and waited. No one came. She stepped back, noting the curtains were closed.

She strolled around to the back of the house. This yard was smaller than the front. Plants were confined to pots on a ten-by-ten redbrick patio. A covered barbecue stood near a sliding glass door.

The curtains were closed here, as well. She knocked anyway. Then waited and knocked again. No one an-

swered. Her heart sank. Was Maconahey at work? She
had no idea what hours a police detective kept. She
swore under her breath, her exhaustion sweeping in to
claim her now. She sank down onto the back step.

Maybe coming unannounced wasn't the wisest thing
she could have done, but she hadn't known if or what
Cade Maconahey knew about Nancy's involvement
with her daughter's abduction. Perhaps he would warn
Nancy. Scare her into hiding. Joanna hadn't been willing to risk that.

She glanced up at the curtain-covered window.
Maybe Nancy was hiding inside this very house. If
she was, it struck Joanna with a punch to the gut that
all of her knocking and bell-ringing and trying to see
in the windows would have put her on red alert.

She swore, then stood up and banged on the door
even harder, listening again for some sound from inside. The house really seemed empty. Felt vacated.
She sank down onto the step again, burying her weary
head in her hands.

Maybe she should find a pay phone and call the
Seattle Police Department to see whether or not Cade
Maconahey was working, whether or not he was even
in town. Her stomach knotted at the thought. Okay
then, not yet. If he didn't return by evening, she'd call.
Meanwhile, she needed to calm down, to shake off the
nerves and tension that threatened to undo her.

She needed to be strong and clear-minded. She
lifted her head and glanced straight ahead, realizing
there was a path that seemed to lead to the park behind
the library. She forced herself up and moving, each
step easier than the last as her sore muscles began to
loosen and respond.

Her heart and thoughts were heavy as she walked

into the park. Watching mothers happily interacting with their children had been a heart-wrenching sight these past six months since losing her daughter, but for the past two weeks such sightings had been unbearable.

She couldn't shake the notion that every baby she saw might be hers. She quashed the awful, dead-end, panic-rousing thought. She had to concentrate on staying sane. The odds that she'd bump into the person who had her baby or that she'd even recognize her own child were too fantastic to calculate.

She'd never seen her own child, had no memories to dredge up, to cling to, to compare.

She moved faster, taking longer strides, grateful that few people seemed to be in the park this afternoon. The walk stole her tension and she noticed, eventually, that it felt cool beneath the trees, peace-giving, the air sweet and clean.

She was even feeling a bit hungry. Glad for the granola bar in her purse, she headed across the springy grass for a picnic table.

A man and his baby beat her to it. As she approached them, she realized the baby was about her daughter's age. Her throat tightened. Tears stung the backs of her eyes, and there was that dreaded thought: *Was this her baby?* Propelled by a force she could not stop, she moved close to the picnic table on which the man had lain the infant.

As she neared, she realized he was changing the baby's diaper. A boy, she saw. Not her child. Not her missing daughter. A cold blast of disappointment blew through her chest.

The baby let out a delightful squeal and kicked his

chubby legs, squirming as the man struggled to get him into a new diaper.

For the first time in two weeks, Joanna smiled, her eyes widening with disbelief. The man was securing his son's diaper with duct tape.

THE SWEATING MAN in the car listened to the phone ringing on the other end of the line between puffs on his cigarette. He drummed his fingertips on the dashboard, growing impatient waiting for the person who paid for his services to pick up.

He knew no answering machine would interrupt. His "boss" didn't believe in them. Weird. The man liked nothing better than electronic gadgets—spent every penny he could get on them. Had a few earmarked in his copy of the latest issue of *Spy Magazine* just waiting for the do-re-mi.

He squirmed, hating the dampness under his arms and all down the back of his short-sleeved sports shirt. Sweat dripped from his bald head onto his face. He swiped it away with the back of his bare forearm. Damn it was hot. Too bloody hot.

The phone continued to ring in his ear. He flicked the cigarette out the open window, then reached for a cold beer from the ice chest behind the passenger seat; the chilled can felt wet and welcome against his heated palm. He pulled the tab, tossed back a swig, then cursed at the car's frigging air-conditioning, which only sputtered in response to his fiddling with it.

He hit the disconnect button on his cell phone. Where the hell was Boss? He tossed back more beer, biting down his impatience, thinking about the incident two weeks ago. The stooges they'd hired to kill Joanna Edwards and her old man had botched it bad.

Barely winged the old guy. The sweating man had reamed them good and sent them into the hospital to finish the job.

But they were too late, arriving just in time to overhear the Edwards woman screaming about her baby girl being alive. That little tidbit had rocked everybody's world. He rubbed the cold beer can across his face.

Shane Addison should have a lock put on his zipper and the key given to his wife. The man was as randy as a rooster and just as indiscriminate. His plans to make it to the White House one day would be shot to hell if the public realized they had another Clinton on their hands.

Talk about screwing yourself. The sweating man grimaced. *If the guy can't control his urges he oughta get himself cut, then he'd be shootin' blanks, like me.*

He dialed the phone number again. Just seven months ago, Addison thought he'd escaped the fire. The daughter Joanna Edwards had borne was DOD— dead on delivery—her body cremated. He narrowed his eyes. What he didn't understand was how old man Edwards had pulled off hiding the baby and convincing everyone that she'd been stillborn. But he had. Apparently even his daughter hadn't known.

Not that that changed anything. Boss wanted the Edwards dame wiped out anyway. She could still tell the world her sordid little story. Grind Addison's political career to so much pulp. She had to be silenced. Permanently.

So far every attempt to get rid of Joanna Edwards had failed. The woman had the lives of a cat. Or sheer dumb luck. But her time was running out. As soon as she revealed who had the kid, he would kill Joanna Edwards himself.

"Hello," Boss answered on the tenth ring.

The sweating man didn't bother with formalities. "She hasn't discovered the tracer in her car yet. I followed her to a house in Auburn. Seems like no one's home though, so she took off on foot into a park behind the house."

"You followed her, of course?"

"No." He wasn't about to get out in this heat. Go traipsing around in public. Risk being seen. Hadn't Boss ever heard of "matter out of place?" "Her car's still parked down the block."

A furious breath hissed in his ear. "She could be meeting someone in that park."

"I don't think so. She went straight to the house. Knocked on the front and back doors. Peered in the windows." The man took another swig of beer, disgusted that Boss didn't give him credit for a whit of brains. If he weren't being paid so well, he'd tell Boss to shove it. "Why do that if she'd set up a meeting in the park? Besides, I've done some checking, found out whose house this is. I thought you'd like to know."

"Tell me."

"Turns out it belongs to a Seattle police detective name of Cade Maconahey."

"A Seattle police detective?" Boss swore. "Why the hell is she visiting a cop?"

"I hoped you'd know."

"No. And I don't like it."

"Maybe she's been spilling her guts. Maybe he believes her story." The man swiped at the sweat on his face again, hoping his questions were making Boss as uncomfortable as he was. "Maybe he's investigating."

"We've got to find out. Can you get a bug in that house?"

The man glanced at the brick house, at the close proximity of the neighbors, and mentally shrugged. After dark. Dead of night, yeah, maybe. "I think so."

"Don't think. Do."

"Yeah, sure, after midnight…sometime."

"Too late. She'll probably be gone by then. I want to know what brought her all the way from Spokane to see this guy. So, the sooner that bug is in place, the better. Like now."

"But the guy's a cop—"

"So, be careful. And quick."

The sweating man disconnected and tossed the cell phone down on *Spy Magazine*. He grumbled, then smiled as an idea occurred to him. "A bug, my Aunt Fanny."

He had a much better way to accomplish his boss's request and it was a legit deduction.

"DUCT TAPE?" Joanna said, amusement strong in her voice. Considering the heaviness in her heart of late, she was amazed that something could strike her as funny as this. But it did. "That's an interesting choice."

"It works." He smoothed the tape in place, not bothering to look up, concentrating on finishing the job before the baby wiggled away from him. His fingers, she noted, were huge, strong, yet his touch seemed gentle, if a bit clumsy for the task.

He scooped up the baby in his large arms and lifted him to his broad chest. His eyes landed on her then—

intense cerulean blue eyes. He was a big man and
unlikely intimidated by anyone. The frankness of his
stare unnerved her. She had the impression he was
trying to read her mind, delving into her soul with that
look.

She blinked and stepped back from him, but
couldn't stop from pointing out the obvious. "You do
realize most disposable diapers have adhesive tabs on
the sides?"

He remained serious, but nodded. "You'd think that
would work, wouldn't you?"

Clearly the reason it didn't work was none of her
business. In fact, none of what he was doing was her
business. She'd butted in out of surprise and dismay.
He had every right to be rude to her. The best thing
she could do was go back and see if Cade Maconahey
had returned.

Instead, she found herself inexplicably drawn to this
man. His appearance, as well as his diapering methods,
intrigued her. There was something about him that
brought to mind a Chagall painting, raw and true, layers within layers, more than met a first glance.

He had a jawful of dirt-brown whiskers, probably a
week or ten days' worth, a large, defined nose, a broad
forehead and lips that turned interestingly up at the
edges. His sienna hair appeared to have a great cut,
but looked as if it had seen a comb the last time his
chin had seen a razor.

One part of her mind busied itself considering
whether or not she could capture him on canvas. The
larger part of her doubted she would ever have the
opportunity. She sensed that he would never sit still
long enough because something about him seemed as
squirmy as the baby.

He held the baby to his shoulder with one hand as though he was holding a football. The baby was grabbing at his daddy's left ear, trying to put it in his mouth, succeeding only in drooling all over his daddy's neck and T-shirt. Likely the baby was teething. Her heart caught. Did this man realize how lucky he was?

"You're a cute little guy," she said to the baby. He reached out for her with his chubby fingers and jabbered something incoherent, smiling a toothless grin. His button nose wrinkled and the inch-long blond down covering his head lifted in a sudden gust of warm air. His eyes were blue, changing to something that might be green. Hazel, maybe.

"He's really cute. What's his name?" she asked, the question surprisingly catching her off guard and cutting through her like a palette knife.

What was her daughter's name?

The man frowned, seeming to sense her distress. "Cody."

"That's darling." Her throat felt tight and hate sloshed in her belly. Nancy and her father had robbed her of even the right to name her own child.

The heat seemed to make her suddenly light-headed. She gripped the picnic table. When she found her daughter, she would change whatever name the little one had been given to Madeleine Rose, her mother's name. Maddy, for short. At the thought, tears threatened again.

"Nice talking with you," she said and spun away, hurrying back through the park.

CADE WATCHED the woman leave. Had he scared her off with his gruffness or the fact that he looked—and probably smelled—like a slob? He tossed the roll of duct tape into the diaper bag. Hell, why did he care what some strange woman thought of him? He wouldn't be seeing her again. But she'd seemed upset by Cody and that tickled his curiosity bone.

Not to mention that she'd stirred his baser male juices. But then it had been a long while since he'd had them stirred, maybe any sexy female would have that effect on him.

Still, something about those emerald eyes of hers intrigued him, something sad and desperate and determined. He watched the sway of her hips as she disappeared around the bend, and his pulse beat a bit faster. Or perhaps it was something about the way that sundress bared her tanned shoulders, inviting a man to caress, to explore—

His mind headed toward a wild fantasy and he caught himself up short, shaking his head. "Oh, brother," he told Cody. "That's exactly the kind of thinking that landed us in this predicament, pal. You'd better take your old dad home before he gets us both in a deeper mess."

Cade gathered up the diaper bag, slung it onto his shoulder and readjusted his hold on Cody. Nothing in the world could make him regret this particular mess enough to give up his son now that he knew about him. Loved him. He kissed the boy's head.

As tough as taking care of a baby was, Cody was worth it. He was the one person in Cade's life who was really *his family*. The first family Cade had ever known or had. That bond couldn't be broken. He would never give up this child, not to anyone for any reason.

His only fear was that Nancy would turn up wanting

to run off with Cody again. Well, if she planned that, she had another think coming. He'd contacted his lawyer and papers were being drawn up now to claim Cody legally. Let her try and get him then. Let anyone.

JOANNA STALKED to a deserted corner of the park beneath a huge maple tree and sank down onto the cool grass, indifferent to whether or not she ended up with grass stains on the white dress. She had to calm down. Get her desolation and despair under control. Anything less, she'd let herself and her daughter down. *Maddy.* Thinking of the baby by name seemed to steal some of the ice around her heart.

She took out the granola bar and forced it down, her thoughts drifting to Bob. She missed him. Missed being able to talk to him about this. But since she'd told him he couldn't be involved, she'd discovered to her surprise how much he had resented her pregnancy, her baby. Perhaps her obsession with the baby? In all fairness to him, she supposed he'd have loved her child, once he got to know her. That was moot now.

If only she'd never met Shane Addison, fallen for his lies. Then none of this would have happened. *Then Maddy wouldn't exist.* She sighed heavily. Of all the things she regretted, her daughter wasn't one of them. She had to move on. Quit lamenting things she couldn't change.

Damn it, Daddy, why?

No, that was the worst direction to move in. If only she knew which path would lead her out of this dark abyss.

She leaned her head against the trunk of the tree and closed her eyes. No one disturbed her and the afternoon stretched into loneliness and lonelier thoughts. Eventually, she became aware that there was a change in the sound of the traffic on the busy road across the way. Rush hour.

Her spirits lifted. Cade Maconahey might be coming home soon. She rose, brushed off her skirt, gathered her purse and turned in the direction of his house. Her stomach clutched as she thought about confronting Nancy's ex-husband. Would it be another dead end? As she walked, she practiced her pitch, running and rerunning in her head what she planned to say to him.

Would he know where Nancy was? Have a clue how she could find his former wife? She strode past the library and crossed the street into the area behind Maconahey's house. Only then did she recall the sense that someone had been following her or spying on her when she left home. She'd forgotten her number-one rule and let down her guard.

Stepping out of the shade of the trees and into the sunlight felt like striding into a spotlight with all eyes drawn immediately to her. Her mouth dried. Her nerves jumped. She scanned the faces of people driving into the parking lot of the library, emerging from their cars, terrified that someone was there to do her harm. No one paid her the least attention.

All the same, she picked up her pace and hurried toward Maconahey's house. As she made the path that led to his backyard, she saw the curtains across the sliding glass door flap in the breeze. The door was open. Her breath caught. Someone was there. Him? Or her?

Joanna forced herself to walk slower. She didn't want to scare anyone off. But when she reached the edge of the patch of lawn she heard a baby crying. Her baby! Maddy! Joanna's pulse leaped and despite all of her self-admonitions to move with caution, she raced over the brick patio and grabbed the curtains.

"Maddy!" she yelled, and swept inside. The room was pitch-dark after the blinding glow of the sun. Her feet hit something slick. Like cloth. She flailed her arms. Tried grasping something, anything, to stop her from toppling. Nothing. Her feet flew out from under her, dropping her hard on her bottom.

The baby continued to cry from somewhere in the house. Joanna struggled to get up. "Maddy!"

"If you don't want to die right where you are, lady, then shut up and put your hands in the air. Now."

Joanna froze. Terror raced through her, over her. She blinked. Her vision focused slowly on a shiny silver object, and as she realized what it was, her heart came up into her throat. She was staring down the barrel of a gun.

Chapter Three

Shane Addison held out his wife's chair. "All those campaign meals of chicken a la king are starting to show on your hips, Kendall."

Kendall Addison felt as if she'd been slapped. Thank goodness they were dining in their own home and not in some public restaurant. Just the same, the servants might overhear. She sank into the straight-backed chair, ignoring the magnificent view of Lake Washington. Her face was hot with humiliation and anger.

Shane sat next to her at the head of the table. His wavy white-blond hair was slicked back off his high forehead, the better to show off his hazel eyes with the thick brown lashes, his nose with the appealing bump in the center, his full mouth that was quick to grin.

Kendall feared that handsome face hid a heart crusty with ugliness. He leaned toward her, keeping his voice low. "We're a team. Don't forget that. The press is calling us the 'golden couple.' That kind of hype can carry us all the way. But not unless we both maintain the image. I mean, it doesn't do me any good to keep in shape if you're not going to do the same."

Kendall fumed. This was not the first time she'd regretted her choice of husbands, but she'd made her political bed a lot of years ago. Her ambitions matched Shane's point for point. First lady of the state would be quite a prize, but she considered it a mere stepping stone. The beginning of a journey that would take them to the top of the political tower. She was in this for the long haul. By God, he'd better be, too.

She leaned toward him. "I'll tell you what, darling. I'll eat like a rabbit. I'll hustle my offending derriere to the gym, work out with Tae Bo, hire Billy Blanks as my personal trainer, if need be...."

"That's my girl." He grinned at her. Getting his way always made Shane happy.

She matched his grin with one a notch brighter. "But only if you give me something in return."

"Anything." He flashed her his "I'll promise you the world, my constituent, whatever you need to hear to cast your vote for me" expression.

She arched an eyebrow at him. "I mean it, Shane. I'll walk out on all of this so fast your head will spin. I'll smear your name from here to the White House and back. You know I can do it."

Beneath his tan, he blanched. His hand snapped around her wrist, his grip viselike, painful. He hissed, "What the hell are you talking about?"

She winced beneath his hold, then embracing her fury, she sneered at him. "Fifteen months ago. Paris. That Edwards woman. Her baby."

He released her and sat back, his mouth in a tight line. "She was a mistake. I told you that."

Kendall rubbed her wrist. "If she were the only slip you'd made during our ten-year marriage we wouldn't be having this conversation. We both know, however, that Joanna Edwards is one in a long line of 'mistakes.'"

"You wound me, Kendall. Really wound me. I'm not the heel you're making me out to be, I swear. I can't believe you'd make me pay the rest of my life for one indiscretion." Innocence draped him like a scarlet scarf on a snowman, fitting, yet a glaring slash against the stark contrast of the truth. She almost laughed that he thought he could get away with pulling this act on her. She knew him too well.

"Don't take me for a fool." Kendall huffed. "If you want us to be known as a golden couple, then treat me like an equal. Treat me with respect. Otherwise, I'm calling it quits, here and now. The divorce won't be pretty."

"Divorce?" The word might be garbage on his tongue. "I won't be divorced."

"Then promise me you'll stop your infidelities for good."

Anger narrowed his eyes and he grabbed for her wrist again. "I swear if you try to divorce me I'll—"

She jerked her wrist out of his reach. "What? See that I meet with a tragic, fatal accident? Just like the ones my sources tell me that you've tried to arrange for that Edwards woman and her bastard child? Nothing more sympathetic than a man widowed unexpectedly, left to raise his two children alone. It's pure political gold."

"Good God, Kendall. You can't really think I'm capable of arranging a murder?" Air whooshed from his lungs. "I don't condone murder...and certainly not as a way to clean up my mistakes."

To her surprise, he looked genuinely shocked. She'd swear he was. But if not Shane, then who? "Well, if it isn't you, and it isn't me, then who has been trying to eliminate that woman? I was told another attempt was made two weeks ago, which ended up costing her father his life.''

Shane swore. ''Are you serious? Someone has actually been trying to kill her...for months?''

''Yes. It's true.''

''My God, who?'' But a name seemed to occur to him. ''Do you think Mel put a contract out on her?''

She shrugged. ''Mel Reagan is *your* hired gun, not mine.''

''He's not a hired gun. He's my right-hand assistant. I told him to take care of Joanna. Pay her off. I did not tell him to kill anyone, and if that's what he thinks I asked of him, he's wrong. I'll correct the situation before anything further happens.'' He extracted his cell phone from his suit-coat pocket.

Kendall touched his arm. ''And what about what I asked of you? Will you stop your humiliating, possibly career-destroying infidelities?''

''I don't want or need anyone but you. Ever. I mean that, Kendall. You can take it to the bank.''

There was an honesty in his gaze she'd never seen. It threw her. Confused her. Could she believe him? About everything? About anything? About Joanna Edwards? The man was such a liar. Even to himself. But then, at times, so was she. It was an idiosyncrasy they had in common.

THE MAN HOLDING the gun leaned sideways and flicked at something on the wall. A bright light flared on, blinding Joanna for the second time in four minutes. Fear brought focus in the next instant. Sprawled on the floor, with the skirt of her dress near the top of her thighs, she made no attempt to rise, no attempt to cover her legs. Her gaze climbed a mountain of a man and recognition swept her.

At the same moment, he and she both said, "You?"

His well-defined, sienna eyebrows lowered in that dark intimidating scowl he'd offered in the park. "What the hell are you doing in my house?"

"*Your* house? *You're Cade Maconahey?*" He hadn't put the gun down, she noticed. Nor relaxed the wide-legged stance that caused his jeans to hug his strong thighs, to outline his very male anatomy.

"Why are you here?" His voice scratched along her nerves like a rusty saw.

She inched her legs together and swallowed, or tried. Her mouth felt full of sand, gritty and dry. "If you'd put down that gun I'd explain."

That seemed to amuse him, in a mean sort of way. "I'll put down this gun when I decide whether or not to call the locals and have you hauled off to jail."

Arrested? She'd expected there might be trouble from this visit, but none that involved her getting carted off in a police car. "For what?"

"Trespassing."

"What? You must be kidding. I wouldn't have come in without knocking if the baby hadn't been crying." As she said this, she realized she could no longer hear the baby from some other part of the house. His house. His baby. Cody. Not Maddy. Her heart sank inside her and dragged her spirits to the floor with her.

"Next thing you'll be telling me is you're a nanny sent by my brother-in-law." His voice dripped with sarcasm. "Give it up. Why did you break in?"

"Break in? The glass door was wide open." Indignation cooled her self-pity and clarified her thoughts.

He'd mentioned his brother-in-law. Joanna frowned, considering what this meant. It hadn't occurred to her that Nancy's ex might have remarried, that Nancy had lied about them still being lovers as well as friends. Lord, she was a fool. She'd so wanted to believe this guy could help, she'd forgotten that Nancy Wheeler was a liar, a betrayer. She could not trust anything the woman had told her. She waved a hand at him. "Would you please put the gun down and listen to me. I really do need to speak with you, Mr. Maconahey."

It was the second time she'd called him by name and that fact finally seemed to register with him. His gaze, like blue smoke, floated over her exposed skin, rousing the sense that he was actually touching her, caressing her. The power of his glance felt so tactile, she flinched. Only then did she realize her skirt was nearly up to her hips.

She flicked it down, and her cheeks flamed, not from embarrassment or decorum, but from her reaction to his smoldering gaze, from her realization of the very real danger she was in at that moment, both emotionally and physically. Being vulnerable seemed to attract men like sight-seers to the Mona Lisa.

The baby began to cry in the other room again. Cade Maconahey reacted as though someone had struck him between the shoulder blades. He jerked around, lowered the gun and headed out of the room and in the direction of the distressed infant.

Joanna blew out a relieved breath and began to rise, helping herself up by an oak kitchen chair that was decorated with a yellow baby's bib and a red adult-size T-shirt. Splotches of multicolored foodstuff painted both items in designs reminiscent of modern

art, a work that might be titled *Moments in Dining* by
Cody Maconahey.

Grinning at the thought, she glanced around the
room. Various baby and adult male clothing layered
floor and furniture and countertops as though a laundry
hamper had exploded.

Beneath the mess she made out oak planking on the
floor, a round oak table beneath a diaper bag and jars
of baby food, a washer and dryer beneath soiled blan-
kets, sleepers, jeans and sweats. She bent over and
picked up the hand towel she'd slipped on when she'd
charged through the glass door. She tossed it onto the
toppling heap already covering the washer lid.

This man could use some help, she mused, some
organization.

The baby's crying grew louder and Cade entered
the room with Cody tucked in the crook of his arm
much as a man would carry a small sack of groceries.
Cade appeared helpless against the onslaught of the
baby's distress.

"Maybe he's hungry," she suggested.

Cade glared at her in surprise. "Why are you still
here?"

"I told you I need to speak with you." Where had
he put the gun? Somewhere safe, she hoped. Somewhere away from the baby.

Cade lifted the baby with both hands, gripping
Cody's chest beneath his tiny underarms. Cody
shrieked in protest. Cade shook his head at Joanna.
"Sorry, can't hear a word you're saying."

She noticed a bottle on the counter. She hurried to
the sink, ran hot water and suds, washed and rinsed
the bottle and filled it with formula, which she quickly
heated in the microwave. Behind her, Cade hummed

off-key to the baby. The baby's cries increased. Cade found the words to the tune he'd been humming, singing softly, with ear-abusing flatness, having apparently forgotten that she was there. Joanna grimaced, but was touched by this man's efforts, by the lengths he'd probably go to appease his son. Even if he was clueless. Cody cried harder still.

She secured the nipple to the bottle and tested the liquid's temperature on her wrist, then turned toward the man and his baby. Cade now held Cody cradled in both arms, rocking him back and forth. Cody continued to squirm and bawl, pulling in gulps of air.

Filling his tummy with air, she thought. For a father, Cade Maconahey seemed overwhelmed by his pint-size son. If not for the baby's distress it would have been laughable. As she sidled up to them, Cody's teary eyes locked on her, then on what she was offering. He gave a relieved snuffle, clamped onto the bottle with both chubby hands and rammed the nipple into his mouth.

The sound of suckling replaced the noisy crying in the kitchen—happy, contented music to her ears.

She felt tension drop from Cade. He pinned her with a stare, but this time it held an amazed and grateful glint. "How'd you do that? *Know* that?"

Instinct, she supposed. It sure wasn't from practice. She shrugged. "It seemed like a good possibility that he was hungry."

He balanced Cody with both hands and motioned Joanna to one of the kitchen chairs. "I appreciate the help. I guess I can spare you a few minutes. What do you need?"

She plucked a pair of Jockey briefs from the chair

with her finger and thumb, flung them toward the washer, and sat. "I need to find Nancy Wheeler."

"Get in line."

What the hell did that mean? "I've come all the way from Spokane today."

His eyes brightened. "From Spokane? Are you her friend from Spokane?"

"Her friend? That is not exactly how I'd qualify our relationship these days. She was my midwife."

He seemed to want to ask her something, but stopped himself. "Go on."

"She told me she called you about my...situation." Had Nancy lied about that, too? His failure to answer fed her doubts. She glanced at the feeding baby and back at Cade. Why did she feel she could trust this man with her deepest secrets and regrets? Something in his warm gaze? His encouraging glances? The way he held that baby?

She decided to give him as pared-down a version as she could manage. "A year and a half ago I was living in France, in Paris, studying art. While I was there, I met an American businessman named Adam Shane. I fell in love, believed everything he told me. I had no reason to doubt him, no experience with rogues and rats."

She leaned toward Cade, noting that the baby had drunk half the bottle. "Aren't you going to burp him?"

Cade's eyebrows flickered. "Burp him?"

"Yes, put him up on your shoulder, thus, and gently pat his back." She mimicked what he should do as she spoke. "If you don't, he's likely to spit up half of what you've fed him."

"He is? Maybe that explains..." He lifted Cody and

began patting his back, each contact like the thump of a paddle on a tom-tom.

"Gently," she reminded him, then smiled. How long had he been doing this? He sure didn't seem to know much about the care and feeding of a baby. She got up and retrieved the hand towel from the washer. She brought it to him and placed it over his shoulder, spreading it, smoothing it with both hands, inadvertently feeling the muscle beneath his T-shirt, the warmth. Their gazes met, colliding like misguided stars. An explosion of unbidden, unexpected sensual heat shot through Joanna. She saw Cade swallow as though he had felt a similar twinge and she stepped back.

He eyed the towel, then her, questioningly.

"My grandmother called it a burp rag. It will save you having to change clothes every time you feed Cody."

Cade laughed, a throaty chuckle that swirled against her ears like some sweetly twanged chord. He seemed almost embarrassed that she'd witness his chagrin, almost ignorant of the zing of sexual awareness that had passed between them. Almost. He gazed at the baby and then at her. "You were telling me about your Paris boyfriend...?"

The moment shattered like hard candy against stone. She nodded. "He left one day without so much as a goodbye to me. When I went to his hotel I was told no one by that name had ever stayed there. I had no idea who Adam Shane really was or where to find him. Everything he'd told me was lies. I spent the next weeks licking my wounds, kicking myself, and learning to write the whole thing off as a bad experience, a valuable lesson in life and men.

"Then I discovered I was pregnant."

As she talked, she straightened the slew of baby-food bottles on the table. "There was nothing to do but come home."

"You could have had an abortion." He said this with the voice of a man who'd seen too much of the world, been hardened by it, and expected everyone to choose the less moral path.

Perhaps if she'd been cynical, or bitter. Perhaps if she hadn't lost her mother when she was ten...but she had. Life was precious to Joanna. All life. She would never have destroyed her baby no matter how it was conceived. Not even though having and keeping her baby had meant putting her art career on hold. "No."

Cade looked at her over his son's head, his wonderful eyes showing respect, admiration for a woman willing to take on the hardships and challenges of raising a child alone, as though he understood personally what that sacrifice entailed.

Did he? Where was Cody's mother? She licked her lips. "I came back to Spokane. Moved back in with my father. Then one day I was watching TV and there he was—Adam Shane. Only his real name was Shane Addison, and he was running for governor of this very state. He was married with two daughters."

And Maddy made three.

The baby emitted a loud burp. Cade gazed at his son in awe, then cradled him on his lap and began feeding him again. "What did you do?"

"At first, I was too stunned to do more than walk around in a daze. Eventually, I decided to do nothing. I wanted nothing more to do with Shane Addison. I didn't want him in my life or in my baby's life. But my father was outraged. He wanted to tell the world.

I dissuaded him of this notion, made him promise on the life of my unborn daughter.

"But he just couldn't stand watching the newscaster on TV praising him, or reading in the newspapers about some charity or other that he'd contributed to. As far as my father was concerned, if Shane Addison had money to throw around at charities, then he'd best remember that charity began at home. He owed his unborn daughter financial support. Dad went behind my back and contacted either Shane himself, or someone close to him."

She blew out a weary, sorrowful breath. "A few days later, someone tried to kill my dad and me in our garage. It was the first of several attempts on our lives."

Cade's eyebrows lifted. "You *are* the friend Nancy called me about." He explained to Joanna why he hadn't come to her aid after Nancy's call, that Spokane was out of his jurisdiction, how without proof he could do nothing legally about investigating a man running for governor.

"I knew that. Dad and I discovered how little could be done when the Spokane police inquired into that first attempt. They promised to investigate, but told us not to get our hopes up. Dad tried telling them it was Shane Addison, but of course, the police need evidence, not accusations. We had none. We realized then and there that I dare not give birth in a hospital. Dad hired Nancy as my midwife. She lived with us for the last two months of my pregnancy and I had thought we'd become friends."

"She's very likable." He gazed at her hard, obviously wondering what had happened to change her opinion of his ex-wife. "When was the last time you saw her?"

"The day we buried my daughter."

"Buried?" He looked stunned, inadvertently hugging Cody, obviously not even wanting to think about anything taking the baby from him. She knew that look, that feeling.

Joanna drew a wobbly breath. "I was having a difficult delivery. I begged them to call an ambulance. But Dad and Nan said it would be okay. The pain was so bad, I don't know what happened, but I passed out. When I awoke, the birth was over and Dad broke the news to me. My daughter was stillborn and Nancy was taking care of the arrangements. Later that week, she picked up the ashes from the mortuary and we buried Maddy in the backyard."

"My God. I'm sorry." His look was so tender it staggered her pulse.

She rushed ahead, fearing she'd wouldn't get it all out. "Nancy left that night. I had no idea where she'd gone, but thought she might have felt somehow guilty that the baby was stillborn. I hadn't heard from her until two weeks ago. She wrote to congratulate me on my plans to marry. I have no idea how she knew. Newspaper maybe. The envelope was mailed from Spokane, but had no return address.

"The day of my wedding, another attempt was made on Dad and me." She told him about the drive-by shooting, her father being wounded and subsequently dying from a heart attack after confessing that her daughter was still alive. "Which is why I'm looking for Nancy. She is the only one who could have made arrangements for someone to adopt my little girl. I have to find her in order to find Maddy."

He lifted Cody to burp him again. Cade's eyebrows were dipped low over his wonderful blue eyes and his expression oozed sympathy and pity.

Joanna wanted neither. "Do you know where I can find Nancy?"

"Not a clue."

Was he lying? Protecting his ex-wife out of some lingering loyalty? "I'll press charges if I don't find her."

"Hey, I'd gladly write up the report."

"You would?"

"Yes."

"Why?"

"Because she's pulled the same kind of disappearance act on me."

"What is that supposed to mean?" Joanna didn't understand. "When did *you* see her last?"

"A week ago."

Joanna's hopes leaped. "Where?"

"Here."

"Here? In Auburn? In this house?"

"Yes."

"What did she want?"

"To tell me about my son. *Our* son."

"Nancy and *your* son?" Joanna frowned and her gaze dropped to the downy-haired baby now curled and sleeping on his daddy's wide chest. "Cody?"

"The one and only."

"But how...?"

He nuzzled the baby's head and gave her a sheepish look that disarmed as well as charmed, a look contrary in every aspect to the size and sternness of his build. "The old-fashioned way."

The old-fashioned way? He'd totally misunderstood

her question. Joanna swallowed against the lump forming in her throat. Her nerves began an underlying hum, like the buzz of low-level electricity. "H-how old is Cody?"

"Seven months, give or take a week."

Joanna reined in the urgency to leap to conclusions, but she couldn't stop herself. Her heart beat a hundred times too fast. Seven months ago, Nancy Wheeler had not been pregnant. But this man seemed to think she had been. How could that be? What could *that* mean? An awful thought occurred and cooled her heated assumptions. Perhaps, *his* Nancy Wheeler was not *her* Nancy Wheeler. Perhaps they were talking about two different women. She needed to be sure, to rein in these wild thoughts. "Do you have any photos of Nancy?"

"Yes." Carefully, Cade stood, holding the baby to his chest. "In my bedroom."

He led the way into the hall and down to the end room. His bedroom was cast in dim light that peeked in through half-closed charcoal blinds. She had the sense of gazing at a cluttered pencil sketch. The area was huge, and she suspected he'd knocked out a wall and combined two bedrooms to make this one.

A sleek, white oak bed and dresser took up one end, a wall-mounted TV and exercise equipment the other.

There was a tangled scent of male cologne or aftershave and baby talc. With his back to her, Cade headed toward his bed. "I'm furious with Nan for keeping Cody a secret. She robbed me of watching him being born, of those first precious months of his life and I can never recover that. But showing up on my doorstep, then slipping off in the middle of the night without so much as a note..."

As he trailed off, she spied four cardboard boxes set on the mattress at the edges of his bed. They were connected with duct tape and formed a makeshift play-pen in the center. He laid the sleeping baby in the space and covered him. Joanna bit back a grin and the urge to suggest that using one of the five-feet long boxes as a bed might have been a better idea.

He walked to a dresser and lifted a photograph. "It's Nan and me at a picnic out back."

Joanna took the photo in her trembling hands. Her vision wobbled. Her knees went weak. She stared at the photo, willing her gaze to steady. On one side of the barbecue, which she'd noticed outside next to the glass door, stood a flame-haired woman hugging a clean-shaven, handsome man in crisp blue jeans and an SPD T-shirt. It took a second to realize this great-looking guy with the dimple in his chin was Cade. She shifted her attention back to the woman. Her breath caught and her body trembled. *His* Nancy was *her* Nancy.

Like a zombie, she walked to the dresser and set the photo down, ignoring Cade's questioning curiosity as she tried to understand how all the pieces of this puzzle fit together. She knew what Cade did not: Nancy Wheeler had not been nine months pregnant, the old-fashioned or any other way, seven months ago.

In the mirror, she saw him reach down and stroke the baby's cheek, a look of such love entered his eyes there was no doubt that Cody had wrapped his tiny fingers around this man's heart.

But for all that Cade Maconahey thought this boy was his own natural son, she knew otherwise. Who was the boy's father then? What game was Nancy playing? And why? She exhaled a trembling breath.

Was Nancy involved in some kind of kidnapping ring? Stealing babies and selling them for profit?

Fear clutched her. *Had she sold Maddy?*

Joanna's head ached with trying to understand, to figure out how the woman she'd known and trusted and considered an honest friend, could involve herself in such a vile practice. Such an illegal practice. But then, she'd never have thought Nancy would lie about Maddy, run off with Maddy.

Joanna turned and her gaze met Cade's. He stepped toward her, speaking softly. "What?"

She opened her mouth, then shut it. How could she tell him? How could she even suggest what she was thinking? No. The theory that Nancy was involved in black-market babies didn't hold water. Granted, she skirted the law, but not for monetary profit. And if she was doing something as illegal as *that,* she'd never involve her ex-husband, the cop.

Then whose child was this?

The possibility sneaked up on her like a mugger, its weapon that awful sensation of bumping into the very person who had her child. This time her mind didn't shove it away. This time her mind embraced it. But was it true? Yes! A voice she'd swear was her father's rang in her head and brought a certainty she could neither explain nor deny. Where else might Nancy have gotten a child of this age?

She slumped against the dresser, grabbed back at its top edge. But it wasn't enough to hold her erect under the enormity of the lies her father and Nancy had told her.

She stared at the baby, knowing in her heart and in that moment that she hadn't given birth to a baby girl at all. She'd delivered a baby boy. A healthy baby boy.

This baby boy with Shane Addison's snowy-blond hair and hazel eyes.

Cody was her son.

She gasped, the realization ripping a sob from her. Her hands flew to her mouth. The room swayed and tilted. Her gaze riveted on Cody. She took a step toward the bed, her hand outstretched to him. Blackness rose at the edges of her vision. She felt the floor opening up, swallowing her, sucking her down.

The last thing she heard was Cade Maconahey's startled cry. "Hey, lady, what's—"

Chapter Four

Joanna awoke to find Cade Maconahey hunkered down, leaning over her. A lock of his dark brown hair grazed his forehead and concern and confusion cooled his cerulean eyes. He brushed hair from her cheek, his fingers warm against her temple, her forehead, his touch surprisingly gentle, his words tender, ''Are you sick or something? Should I call an ambulance?''

''No. I'm—'' Joanna struggled to sit up. He'd placed a pillow beneath her head, she realized. A wave of dizziness swept her, passing quickly, but she feared the cause of her distress might never pass.

His eyebrows twitched questioningly. He expected an answer, an explanation. How did she tell this man that she'd just had her whole world rocked, the very foundation of all of her truths turned to quicksand? That the truth she'd discovered would destroy his world?

She pushed up to a sitting position and closed her eyes, grasping for emotional strength. ''I—I haven't been eating much the last couple of weeks. That, combined with the heat...well, I got a little light-headed. Must have fainted.''

''Are you sure that's all?'' He studied her face.

"Yes." If he saw through her lie he didn't show it. "I could fix you some scrambled eggs."

The thought of food set her stomach churning. "I'm not sure I could get them down."

"You need to try." He reached for her hand and helped her to her feet. She swayed, falling into him. With lightning reflexes Cade caught her, gathering her to him, his arms circled her, supported her, his broad hands warm and clutching at her waist.

Joanna's palms pressed his chest, and she felt pliant, muscled flesh beneath the thin cotton fabric of his shirt. His heart pulsed against her fingertips and an unbidden warmth coursed through her veins and eased the sickening chill in her belly. There was something so comforting, so calming about his embrace, she wanted to lose herself in it, to nestle there until she could control the urge to grab her baby and run, until she could compose herself enough to think, to digest and process her new knowledge, until she could make decisions with a clear head.

Terror kept her ever aware that Shane Addison wanted her and her baby dead. If not for that, the moment she'd awakened she'd have been tempted to scoop that baby off the bed and dash out into the night. But God knew what awaited them there.

She began to tremble and Cade said softly, "Hey, hey, now. What's got you so spooked?"

She shook her head, pressing her nose into his soft shirt, pulling in the scent of baby and soap and something that was purely male, purely Cade. Instead of unnerving her further, this awareness lent her myriad comfort.

But knowing what she knew, she had no comfort for him. She couldn't bring herself to look at him, or answer him. Likely he wanted to be rid of her, with her wild accusations about his ex-wife, about the front-runner for governor of this state. After all, it was obvious he was overwhelmed trying to care for Cody. He certainly didn't need or want an insane woman with a tendency toward fainting spells on his hands.

But the one thing Joanna would not do was leave. Not without her son. And when she did manage to convince Cade Maconahey that *his* son was actually *her* son—what then? How would she ever keep her child and herself safe in a world where Shane Addison called the shots?

She drew a ragged breath. Maybe the safest place for her son was right here. With Cade. The thought of leaving Cody without claiming him tore through her heart, threatening to knock her to the floor again.

"Come on, let's get something to eat before junior here wakes and reclaims his reign of the castle." He grinned at her, placing his arm across her shoulder, his hold just strong enough to keep her erect. "Besides, I need some sustenance—or I'll be fainting next."

She glanced at her sleeping son and her feet moved toward him of their own volition. The pressure of Cade's fingers on her shoulder stopped her, sobered her, and forced her to rein in the soul-wrenching ache to hold her baby and gulp down the sobs that crowded the back of her throat.

If she loved that boy, and she did, then she would do the best thing for him, no matter how badly it hurt. And God, walking away from her son was the worst hurt she'd ever felt.

Woodenly, she allowed Cade to lead her into the kitchen. A part of her wanted to soak up his tenderness, his kindness, anything to blunt the pain that seared her every pore. He led her to a chair. She sat, the hard surface as jarring as the reality that she would use this man as she had used Bob, if she needed to.

Had she learned nothing in the past two weeks? Would she always revert to old patterns when the going got tough? No. It was time she stood up to the devils in her world and took her best shot at conquering them. Her son needed her to do that. For him, she found the strength inside herself to try.

But how?

Instead of scrambled eggs, Cade picked up the phone and ordered fast food from a local deli. At her surprised look, he shrugged and spread his hands in a gesture meant to draw her attention to the disaster that was his kitchen. "The truth of the matter, as you can see, is that I don't have enough clean pans or dishes to cook. You'd probably never believe this, but usually I'm the most fastidious guy you'd ever meet. Somehow this week I've lost the time and the energy to keep on top of the mess."

Conversely, staring at the chaotic room brought order to Joanna's thoughts. Her mind swept out the clutter of self-pity, mopped away the muddy self-predictions of a dire future and dumped into a mental dustbin her debilitating fear. There might just be a way that she could buy the time to soften this blow for Cade, time to get to know her son, time for Cody to get to know her. "You could use some help."

He laughed. "Tell me about it."

"I could help...if you'd like."

He frowned, churning the suggestion, trying to understand her offer. He shoved at the hair falling across his forehead as if he'd only just noticed it. "What are you suggesting?"

She gathered her courage. Everything she cared about was right here, under this roof. "Well, I—I noticed you have a guest room. I thought maybe I could stay and help with the laundry, the dishes, the dusting and...Cody."

His frown deepened and a new fear snaked around her heart. She had to convince him. Make him see this was the best thing for both of them. She recalled his crack about his brother-in-law sending her as a nanny, and slightly shifted the direction of her argument. "Look, I realize you don't know me from Adam, but if you had some other source of help you'd have called on it by now."

"Okay, I'll concede the obvious." He leaned his hip against the counter, his pose not unlike a Rodin sculpture, bronzed and beautiful in that moment. She could not look away. He said, "But I don't like the idea of strangers in my house, around my son. That's why I haven't hired anyone to help."

"That's why you're in this mess."

"Touché." He sighed. "Even if I decided to consider your offer—and I'm not saying that I am—I wouldn't trust someone with my son or my house without references. Do you have references?"

She touched the baby-food jars she had aligned earlier and considered his question. "Any references I might offer—and I could offer dozens—would be prejudiced and come from friends and relatives and former employers that you don't know. The only friend we share is Nancy."

"Unfortunately, neither of us know where to find her at the moment. And I don't think we can trust she'll turn up any time soon."

"Really?" Why was he so certain of that? She

didn't pursue this line of thought. She needed to convince this man and she needed to do it now. "You're a police detective. Don't you ever have a gut instinct when something is right?"

He arched an eyebrow at that. "As a matter of fact, I do. All the time."

"Then it should be telling you now that I'm sincere and trustworthy and honest."

A peculiar look crossed his face, half amusement, half skepticism. "Don't you have a life, a job in Spokane?"

"No. My life stopped two weeks ago. It won't start again until I claim my child."

"What about that wedding you mentioned?"

She didn't answer, just shook her head. Now was not the time to explain that. "I need to find Nancy. You and Cody are the only links I have to her."

He scrubbed his whiskered jaw.

Her heart hammered so hard she could hear it. Could he? "You really need a hand around here. This place is a virtual germ magnet. You don't want Cody to get sick, do you?"

"What if Nancy never shows up?"

Joanna was no longer sure she cared one way or the other about Nancy. She'd found her baby. She didn't need Nancy's confirmation. But she couldn't tell him that. Not yet. "Do you really think that's a possibility?"

"Naw." He shoved at his hair again. "I don't like the game she's playing. She has a lot to answer for and I guess you have a right to some of those answers. But she loves kids. She'll show up in her own sweet time."

"And meanwhile…?"

His nostrils flared as he blew out a breath. "Meanwhile, you can stay the night and we'll see how tomorrow goes. But if anything hits me wrong, you'll leave. No arguments." The hard glint in his eyes said he didn't manhandle women, but he would make an exception if he wanted her to leave and she refused. He stuck his hand out to shake hers. "Agreed?"

She took his hand and they shook on it. "Agreed."

"Good. 'Cause my main priority is my son."

"Don't worry. Cody's *my* top priority, too."

The doorbell rang. Joanna's first thought was that Shane Addison or his henchmen had found her and her son. "Don't answer it."

"Are you kidding?" Cade shoved away from the counter. "That'll be our food."

The stark fear in her emerald eyes worried him. In his gut he knew he'd done the right thing for her in allowing her to stay on a trial basis, but had he done right by his son? Would he regret this decision? He'd better not. He would keep a close eye on her. Tomorrow morning first thing, he'd have Harley Taggert, a co-worker, contact someone in the Spokane Police Department to authenticate or disavow her story about the alleged murder attempts on her life.

Sure he had Nan's word that someone had once tried killing this woman, but after this latest stunt, he trusted Nan as much as he did the lie that the cost of postage stamps wouldn't rise. He increased his steps to coincide with the increased ringing of the doorbell. What if it turned out that Joanna wasn't lying or exaggerating about someone wanting her and her baby dead? That someone was gunning for her? Cade smacked his fist against his palm. If it were true, he'd send this woman packing. He would not put Cody in the line of fire.

But just the possibility of someone after an innocent woman and child sent fury burning through him. He liked Shane Addison. Planned to vote for him. The man was running a campaign on family values, but if there was something Cade couldn't stomach it was phonies and liars.

Not to mention murderers.

Was Shane Addison all three?

"I'm coming." Wanting to strangle the person at his door, Cade flipped on the foyer light, and was struck by the clutter that had reached even this tiny area. God, how had he managed to upend his orderly house like this in such a short time? The doorbell rang again, with an insistent chiming that would wake the baby if the caller didn't stop this minute.

Too late. He heard Cody begin to cry. He moaned. He would have to put a sign on the front door, or disconnect the bell for a while.

As he opened the door with one hand, he dug his wallet out of his back pocket with the other. To his surprise, it wasn't the food delivery person on his doorstep, but his ex-brother-in-law. "Ted? Was I expecting you?"

Ted shook his head, his expression was an unsettling mix of grimness and excitement. He shoved past Cade and into the house in that nervous-energy way that juries often mistook for passionate sincerity in his summation of a case at trial.

He spewed, nonstop, "I probably should have phoned, all the way here I kept telling myself that, but then I'd remember there wasn't anything you could really do, having no one to watch the baby, so I de-

cided I'd better come in person because then I could
tell you face-to-face and—''

Cade clamped a hand on the smaller man's shoulder, ending the diatribe and finally getting his attention. Ted plucked the baseball cap off his thatch of
wavy red hair and held the brim in both hands at chest
level like a little boy who'd been caught throwing
rocks at his classmates. There was something about
Ted that would always be boyish. In some it might be
charming. In Ted it was annoying.

"What the hell is it?" Cade growled, his impatience
and concern near snapping.

Ted swallowed and barely gasped, "Nancy."

Cade's heart dipped. "Has something happened to
her?"

"Well, see, that's just it, when I got there and then
saw what they'd done, I mean it's bad, man, really
bad." His blue eyes glazed and he seemed to be seeing
beyond Cade's shoulder, something distant, inside his
head. "It's just so bad."

Cade squeezed Ted's shoulder again, silencing him.
"Come into the kitchen."

Cade knew he'd never get anywhere unless he
calmed Ted down enough to be coherent. He ushered
Ted into the kitchen, surprised to see Joanna gone. But
he realized the baby was no longer crying and guessed
she'd gone to him. At least her instincts were good.
He got down the brandy bottle and poured a shot,
which he handed to Ted.

In the kitchen light, Ted's complexion was the color
of sour cottage cheese. Whatever the hell had brought
him here really had him shaken. He pointed to the
chair Joanna had vacated. "Sit down and drink that
brandy. All of it."

When he'd drained the glass, Cade refilled it. Then he joined Ted at the table with his own glass of brandy. "Now, nice and slow, buddy, tell me what's going on?"

JOANNA ENTERED Cade's bedroom, as irresistibly drawn by the cries of her baby as Van Gogh had been drawn to his subjects. She found a light and moved toward the bed, speaking as she approached, keeping her voice low, not wanting anyone expect Cody to hear her. "Shh. It's okay, darling, Mommy's here, and she's not going anyplace ever again without you."

The sound of her voice stilled the baby's cries. He lifted his head and peered up at her. A smile parted his lips and her heart skipped a happy beat. Tears dotted his lashes like dew on rose petals. This was the most precious face she had ever seen, bar none.

She wanted to devour her son, to cleave him to her, to forge the bond that she'd been denied at his birth, that after all this time might now never be formed. Urgency gripped her. It also frightened her. She didn't want to scare Cody, to smother him as her father had often smothered her after they'd lost her mother.

"Slowly," she cautioned herself. Her heart thudded her rib cage, throbbed in her ears. Joanna reached out a finger to touch the tears on Cody's lashes, to feel those lashes damp and long, to trace the rounded curve of his precious cheek.

Cody had other ideas. He squeaked in delight and grabbed her finger in his tight, tiny fist. A streak as hot and fierce as fire shot up Joanna's arm and straight into her soul—an incendiary jolt as though she'd been struck by lightning. The seven-month-old crust of ice that coated her heart evaporated in a pulse beat, in a child's touch, *her* child's touch.

A small laugh burbled up in her. Cody responded with another squeal, his grip tightening as though he were claiming her without waiting for her to claim him first. Tears filled Joanna's eyes, tears of joy, tears of release, tears of a mother whose child has found his way home.

Joanna, burning with life and love, lifted the make-shift playpen and sank to the mattress. She gathered Cody into her arms, lifting him to her chest, his head nestled in the curve of her neck, his tiny body pressed into her loving embrace. "Oh, oh, oh." The cries came out of her in soft whimpers, and tears streamed down her cheeks. "Thank you, God, for this precious child, for keeping him safe and well."

She rocked back and forth, kissing her son, inhaling his milky, baby-lotion scent, imbuing herself with it, memorizing the shape of his head, the texture of his skin, the downy softness of his hair. He felt so right in her arms, as though she'd held him there before, knew him, and yet, how impossible was that? Her body vibrated, in tune with some inner song set off by this child, who lay against her unresisting, seeming content in a whole new way, perhaps recognizing her as she recognized him, a lifeblood acknowledgment, a spiritual reuniting.

The sensation was brief-lived. Cody squirmed, pushing against her hold, and she recalled her promise to herself not to smother him, not to hang on to him so tightly that all he wanted was to break free—as she'd wanted so often to break free from her dad's silent proprietorship.

She lowered him onto her lap, realizing for the first

time just how heavy his diaper felt. He was soaked. Her dress had a damp patch. She chuckled quietly. "So, you've initiated me, huh? I guess we'd better change you."

She found a plastic sackful of diapers next to the bed, laid Cody on the mattress and plucked at the duct tape Cade had used as tabs, smiling at the memory. The baby squirmed and kept trying to roll over, with, she assumed, every intention of scooting away. Holding him down on his back and trying to get the diaper off and clean him was like handling a greased pig.

She laughed again. "No wonder Cade has been having so much trouble keeping ahead of you. You've got the energy of three puppies, Cody."

Cody. It was not a name she'd have chosen, but she liked it. It suited him. She decided not to change it. As she wrestled to keep him from squirming free, she studied her son as she might a newly discovered artist, looking for imperfections, finding none. All toes and fingers accounted for, she turned him this way and that, deciding he was incredible. Flawless.

From the top of his silky blond hair to his wide-set greenish-gold eyes and bud of a nose, to his small, shell-shaped ears that hugged his head, to the dimples above his round little bottom and chubby knees, to the tip of his big toe, he was a masterpiece.

"I knew you'd be wonderful," she cooed. "You have your grandpa's ears." She touched the tiny ears as she spoke. "And my mouth and chin." The realization pleased her, awed her. She thought of the portrait she'd completed a month earlier. *Baby of Mine*. Luna thought it was wonderful. The best thing she'd ever done. The baby she'd painted was a startling match for this little guy—because, she realized, she'd used her own baby pictures for the model. "In fact, you look much as I did when I was your age. Someday I'll show you the photographs."

Cody couldn't care less. With the new diaper in place, he was twisting free and wiggling away. Chuckling, she caught him and pulled him into her arms again. She whispered, "Oh, I could hold you like this forever...my Cody."

Unfortunately, that wasn't an option. For the moment, she would have to content herself with whatever time Cade Maconahey allowed her with *his* son. It was enough now that she'd found him, that the vast hole and tearing loneliness inside her had gone.

Her fingers brushed the hem of his T-shirt; it was wet. "You need a dry shirt, maybe sleepers, my sweet darling, but the question is, do you have any?"

"DO YOU HAVE any clean clothes for this little guy?" Joanna strode into the room carrying Cody with an ease that struck Cade as natural, a natural-born mother. She'd be great with her own child, her Maddy, he thought. When she found her.

A frown chased the thought. Joanna was standing stark still, eyeing Ted with a mixture of terror and confusion.

"This is Ted Wheeler," Cade told her. "My ex-wife's brother."

Ted and Nancy looked a lot alike. Cade saw that register in Joanna's green eyes, saw her body shift between rigid to relief and back to a different kind of tension. He thought he understood and made a decision. "Ted, this is Ellen Donahue."

It was a name he'd used recently undercover. Joanna glanced at him sharply, questioningly. He tried conveying a look that said, "Let me do the talking and just back me up." He wasn't sure she understood. It wasn't much of a lie anyway and he could always laugh it off with Ted should she give him away.

Ted filled in the blanks for him. "So, you took my advice and found someone to help, huh?"

"Yeah."

Joanna said, "Cody needs a change of clothes. Where might I find that?"

"The dryer," Cade said.

"Of course. Excuse us." She strode past both men.

Ted watched her appraisingly. Despite his upset over his sister, the guy appreciated a great-looking woman when presented with one.

Just one more thing that annoyed Cade about this man. He shook his head. "Now, what is it that has you so blown away, Ted?"

Ted took a swig of his brandy and swiped at his mouth with the back of his jacket sleeve. "It's Nan's place, man. It's been dumped upside down. Trashed."

Cade thumped his own glass down on the table. "What?"

Ted was nodding hard. "Yeah, like someone was looking for something, you know? I mean, what could Nan have that someone would want so badly they'd tear apart her apartment?"

Worry shot through Cade. Worry for Nan. For Cody. For himself. He glanced at Joanna. She was hunkered down, hugging Cody to her hip with one hand, digging through clothes in the dryer with the other. Had she heard? Was she pretending she hadn't? He could see the tension in her shoulders.

Ted lamented, "I mean, man, what has Nan gotten herself into?"

What indeed? Cade didn't like this, didn't like it at all. Was whoever had upended Nancy's apartment looking for a way to find Joanna's daughter? To find Joanna, too?

He had no choice. As soon as Ted left, he'd send her packing. Tell her to stay the hell away from him and his son.

Chapter Five

Cade watched Cody grabbing for Joanna's taffy-colored hair, smiling at her, already comfortable with her. He regretted that it would be a short-lived relationship, regretted that his son would again be losing another mother figure in such a brief span of time.

It couldn't be helped.

He rubbed his weary eyes and returned his gaze to Ted. He was used to this man's tendency to blow something small into a big deal. He had no such affliction. He needed facts. Not suppositions. "Did you call the police?"

"Yeah. Sure." Ted nodded, shoving his fingers up through his red hair, making it stand on end like spikes of the fire that fed his nervous energy. "The Issaquah cops showed up. Took a report. Said they'd check for fingerprints, but that it was probably someone who knew the person living in the apartment hadn't been there lately."

Cade took a sip of brandy. He kept his voice calm, reasonable. "That is a possibility."

"I know," Ted said in a low tone. He glanced nervously at Joanna, as though rethinking spilling his guts in front of a stranger. But Cade wanted Joanna to hear what Ted had to say. It would save him recounting it later.

Ted all but whispered, "And I might believe that if Nan hadn't run out on her kid. If she'd given one of us some idea where she was going. Where to reach her. I'm worried, man. Have you heard from her?"

"No. Nothing yet." Cade sighed. "I would have called you."

"Yeah, well..." He glanced at the messy room. "You've had your hands full, you know?"

"I know. But that'll get straightened out." Of course, with him about to send Joanna packing, he wasn't sure when or how the place would get put to right. "I'll call you the minute Nancy contacts me."

The doorbell rang again. Their food. Cade rose, gesturing with his head toward the interruptive ringing. "Meanwhile, you're welcome to share our dinner."

"Oh, God, what time is it?" Ted glanced at his wristwatch and swore. "Oh, man, I'm late for an appointment." He plunked his baseball cap on and went to the door with Cade. "I'll let you know if the police turn up any fingerprints or anything."

"Do that." Cade would check with the Issaquah police himself in the morning. He had his own source there. He didn't need a report from Ted, but following up on the police's investigation would keep Ted out of trouble for a while.

"DO YOU KNOW why someone would want to search Nan's apartment?" Cade asked the question both had avoided as they had tended to Cody and gotten him down for the night, dished up the fast food and eaten their salads. "What could they have been looking for?"

"What do you think?" Joanna lifted her head, pushing her caramel tresses back from her face, tucking a lock behind one delicate ear. Her green eyes were narrowed and he saw hesitation there, leeriness. She said, "You know her better than I do."

Cade had hoped to open this subject so that when he asked her to leave tonight, she would realize why it was necessary. But it appeared she was going to make him pull it out of her. He dropped the subtlety. "Do you think it has anything to do with Shane Addison?"

"Do you?" Her gaze met his and he realized with an inward jolt, a mental shake, that something had changed about this woman since he'd found her sprawled in his kitchen earlier this evening. The haunted, desperate glint was gone from her eyes. What had changed so dramatically in her in that short time?

Cody, he realized. Missing her own child, she'd immediately been taken in by his son. A baby without a mother, a mother without a baby. A perfect fit all around. But he couldn't fault her. Cody had had the same effect on him.

Nan had stolen her daughter, now he was going to rip her away from his son. Damn. How much could the woman take? He really hated this. But how could he put his son in the kind of danger she'd described living with the past eleven months?

He couldn't. No way. She would understand. If Cody were her son, she wouldn't willingly subject him to anything that threatened his life. But given her recent fainting spell, he couldn't tell her to leave before he'd made sure she'd eaten.

As they ate and chatted, Cade felt a calmness of mind and spirit—that had deserted him eight days earlier—returning. Joanna asked him about the yard, whether or not he took care of it himself or hired someone to do it. "I do it myself. What downtime I have, I spend on my roses. As you saw, there aren't many bushes, but those I have are tended with loving care."

"Those are roses in the pots out back?"

"Starts." He grinned. "My garden shrank in size accordingly as my duties with the department grew."

She returned his smile with a warm one of her own. "I don't have a green thumb, unless I accidentally smear paint on it. I envy anyone who can make things grow."

"What I like about gardening," Cade said between sips of milk, "is that plants respond according to the attention given them. There's never any complaints, no reproaches, no tears if I forget to call when I'll be late, no feelings of guilt if I forget a birthday or anniversary."

God, he wondered, startled at his outburst, *where had that come from?*

"That bad, huh?" She stabbed a piece of teriyaki chicken with her fork and lifted it toward her full lush mouth. A mouth that looked as though it could devastate a man.

"Is that why you and Nan—? Oh, God, never mind." She blushed, a lovely pink lighting her creamy cheeks. "I'm sorry. That's really none of my business."

He frowned, amazed still that he'd blurted out something so personal, further confounded by the desire he felt for her, and his desire to tell her even more. Why? What was it about this woman that had him tangled up in knots, yet opening up and baring his soul? He didn't even know her. Maybe it was the rapt way she listened that made it easy to talk to her, easy to let his guard down.

On the other hand, revealing certain bits about his private history might get her to do the same. He realized he wanted very much to know more about Joanna Edwards. "I'm surprised Nan didn't tell you."

Joanna chewed the piece of chicken and swallowed. "She did mention you were a workaholic."

"Did she also mention that I was raised in state institutions? No conventional family for me. No role-model parents. If you look up the word *loner* in a dictionary, you'll find my ugly mug."

She made a face at him.

"It's true. It was one of the things Nancy hated about being married to me. I never learned to be part of a pair."

This confession seemed to affect her in some way he could not fathom. She reached to touch his hand, but stopped short of doing it. Compassion shone in her eyes. It sent a sudden warm zing through his heart, and roused an unbidden, fierce need to protect her in a way he'd thought he'd never feel for anyone but his son.

The feeling floored him. He lacked that protective gene other cops had. But here it was, crashing down on him, unexpected, startling, insurmountable. How could that be? Cade, the loner—who was best at covering his own butt? Who chose undercover work so as not to have to be responsible for a partner? So as not to have to count on anyone but himself? No way. And yet, this new and odd sensation consumed him.

He ate without tasting, not daring to look at her anymore. His mind ached with confusion. Should he be leery of trusting this woman as quickly as he had? Or did the fact that he found her devastatingly appealing scare him? Was that why he'd decided to toss her out so quickly, based on unconfirmed suspicions? Was he reconsidering now because of his attraction to her? Or his son's newfound attachment to her?

He needed to think about this logically—something he normally did without effort. But, then, this was the first time he'd been personally involved, the first time trouble had come knocking on his own front door.

Mentally stepping back and viewing the situation from that perspective, he discovered he hadn't been objective. Nancy, he supposed, not Joanna, had placed Cody and him in the middle of whatever mess she had landed in. It might have nothing to do with this Edwards woman. And knowing Nan, sooner or later, she would show up again, bringing that trouble with her.

So how could he ensure his son's safety? Joanna's safety? He'd always believed in the sageness of keeping his friends close and his enemies closer. This practice had saved his butt more times than he could count. Since Joanna's enemy might now well be his enemy, thanks to Nan, he would be wise to keep her close, in order to keep Addison or his henchmen closer.

But could he manage this if he couldn't retain his objectivity?

"Why don't you clear the dishes while I start a load of laundry and fold the clothes in the dryer?" Joanna suggested, rising.

CADE CARRIED her suitcase into the guest room. It was a mini-version of the master bedroom, mono chromatic in color with an austere queen-size bed and six-drawer dresser against one wall beneath an oval mirror.

Apparently he'd redone the house since his divorce, Joanna thought. Nancy tended to like frills and pastels. If it were up to Joanna, she'd have added a touch of ultramarine blue or crimson, a focus of color and warmth.

Cade set her suitcase on the bed. "I have a contractor coming in the morning to give me an estimate on turning this room into a nursery."

She glanced sharply at him, her mouth drying with guilt. He was making a home for Cody, not only in his heart but in his house. The guilt spread to her throat, her chest. She forced herself to smile. "I guess he can't sleep in that makeshift bed forever."

"Nope. I'm going to deck this all out." His eyes gleamed with an inner vision of a future he anticipated. A future she would one day destroy.

She should tell him the truth now. Not let him get attached to her son more than he already was. But how could she convince him without proof? She had no photographs of Nancy to confirm that his ex-wife hadn't been pregnant at the time of Cody's birth. No birth certificate. No physical evidence.

They would have to have a DNA test taken. Cade might refuse.

But even if she convinced him, even if he conceded that Cody was her son and not his, even then, there would still be Shane Addison to deal with. The only way she could see to keep her son safe was to go on pretending Cody was Cade's child. Her heart ached for all three of them.

Cade stepped toward the door. "I think I'll, er, hit the sack and, er, I guess I'll see you in the morning."

It was the worst night of her life. Her son was in the next room and she couldn't go to him. Her heart hurt, her conscience nagged. She was going to hurt a very nice man and could see no way around it.

The baby's crying woke her.

She shot out of bed and into the hallway, not stopping for a robe. She found Cody in the middle of Cade's bed, the cardboard playpen back in place. "Oh, sweetie, what's wrong with my little man?"

Cody gazed at her and cried harder. Talking softly, moving swiftly, she lifted the barrier and sank to the mattress, gathering her son into her arms. "I'll bet you're hungry, huh?"

She checked his diapers, but discovered they were dry and secured with duct tape. Cade appeared in the doorway.

Except for the baby bottle, he looked fresh from the shower, his hair damp and curly, his face shaven and smooth, his jaw strong, dimpled, his body naked except for a pair of blue and white Jockey briefs.

She lifted her eyes and swallowed over the lump growing in her throat. The air between them seemed to sizzle. Her gaze slammed into his chest, a broad, well-developed expanse of male flesh lightly brushed with burnt-sienna hair that sprang from the skin between his nipples and grew dark and thick on his belly, disappearing from view into the waistband of his shorts.

She lifted her eyes again, the knot in her throat larger. "Cody. I heard him crying."

She tried hugging the baby to her, but he had seen the bottle and was wriggling and reaching for it, making loud noises. Cade grinned at her, and for a moment she thought it was because she'd used this excuse before to charge in where she had no right.

Belatedly, she realized his smile was full of sensual appreciation and nothing more. He brought the bottle to Cody, but his eyes never left her. His gaze dropped to her bare feet then climbed her bare legs all the way to the hem of the bikini panties and up the body-hugging tank top she wore.

Heat, different and disconcerting, started in her belly and swirled through her blood, sending shards of something electric and sweet to every nerve in her body.

"I have to shower. Here. Here's your baby." She scrambled to her feet, gently but firmly thrust Cody into Cade's arms, and dashed from the room. Cade's warm chuckle followed her into the hallway.

She gathered jeans and a T-shirt, clean underwear and sandals and headed into the main bathroom. She waded through scattered towels, dropped sleepers, big and teeny socks to the tub on the end wall. She smiled and felt a warm confusion of emotion. How had one man and one baby turned this place upside down in one short week?

She pulled the shower curtain aside. Baby shampoo stood on the rim. In the bottom of the tub there was a tiny sponge. Her pulse quickened and her throat thickened. Would she get to bathe her baby today? The possibility hurried her through her shower and into her clothes. She left her hair wet, added some mascara and lip gloss and, carrying an armload of laundry, followed her nose toward the aroma of coffee.

Cade was seated at the table with Cody on his lap. He was feeding him baby cereal, getting more on the baby's face than into his little, eager mouth. The sun shone through the sliding glass door, a soft angel light surrounding them. The sight clutched her heart. Cade's gaze met hers and she felt something warm and unbidden spiraling the length of her, saw something like need in those eyes, a male need, raw and enticing, that roused a thrumming need of her own.

Her pulse skipped. Her mouth watered. She couldn't look away. Not from her son. Not from Cade. He was fully dressed now, in jeans and a polo shirt in a beige hue that was a soft compliment to his tanned skin and coffee-brown hair.

Coffee. She shook herself. Coffee. She needed coffee.

"Good morning…again." Cade's grin was sensuous, teasing.

"That coffee smells great." She tore her gaze from his, crossed to the washer and dryer and dropped the load of clothes on the floor.

Cade said, "There's lots more."

Uncertain whether he meant coffee or dirty laundry, she didn't answer. She found the coffeemaker on the dish-clogged counter and one clean mug standing beside it, waiting for her. Pleased at the gesture, she filled it and spun back to the best sight in the world. These two gorgeous males.

Cade's gaze found and held hers. "I didn't know how you like it."

Like what? she wondered, her mind responding to the heat smoldering in his eyes. "How I like what?"

"Your coffee. Sugar? Cream?"

She smiled. "Black."

"Me, too." Cade shoved more cereal between Cody's parted lips. The baby was looking at her and not the spoon. Mushy cereal smeared his little mouth.

Cade dabbed at it with a kitchen towel. From the look of his laundry he must have been using his shirts before she told him about the burp rag. He was a quick study, she thought, taking a sip of coffee. And he made a decent cup of java.

Cade said, "I have to go up to Issaquah this morning. I want to check out Nan's apartment."

The subjects of Nancy and the break-in erased the warm coziness she'd been feeling. She hadn't allowed herself to dwell on that last night. Didn't want to deal with it then or now. But the chances that it didn't somehow involve her were remote. She frowned. "Are you asking me to go with you? Or to stay here and work on the cleanup?"

"I'm asking you to stay here and wait for the contractor." He glanced at the baby, then back at her. "And to watch Cody."

She lifted her eyebrows, surprise pinging through her. She hadn't expected this level of trust from Cade. Most people, most cops, wouldn't entrust their child to a woman whose baby had been stolen. Not without at least considering she might run off with his child. Had he considered that?

"Sure." She took another swallow of coffee. "What's your contractor's name?"

"Dale Fast. He'll be here at ten, and he already knows what I want done, so mainly he'll be measuring and checking for the cost of structural changes."

By NINE, Cade was gone and Cody was fast asleep on the king-size bed. She went through the house opening drapes and collecting abandoned articles of clothing. She made one last tour to be sure she hadn't missed anything.

With the sun pouring in and the laundry no longer hiding most of it, she saw it was a charming house. The floors were all hardwood. The living-room fireplace was the same redbrick used outside. An oak mantel had been added and bookshelves inset on either side.

There was a stereo on one of the shelves and CDs on another, his tastes running from jazz, she noted, to classical. His furniture was a mix of sleek modern and leather. Here, as in the rest of the house, Cade had gone with monochromatic hues. To Joanna, the effect was simple clean lines without any warmth or focus— a painting conceived, undefined, just waiting for the artist's stroke.

The doorbell rang.

Joanna jumped. All the comfort of a moment before gone in a wink. Her nerves came alert, honed by eleven months of living in sheer terror, but her mind sought denial. Had Cade forgotten something? Could it be the contractor arriving early?

She checked the small chrome clock on the mantel. Nine-fifteen. Would the contractor be this early? She conceded it was possible, but approached the door with caution. Her heart picked up speed with every step. "Who is it?"

"Dale Fast, ma'am."

She reached for the knob, then stopped herself. There was a peep hole in the top half of the door. Joanna peered through it. Two men stood on the porch. One was tall and stocky, his bulk from muscle not fat. Sweat dripped from his bald head and trickled down his face like rain on a windowpane.

The other man, lean, average height, with thick black hair, was turned away from her. He checked the street, then gazed back at the door and then the street in both directions, as though on lookout. The fine hair at her nape stood on end. He shifted toward the door again and she got a first good look at his face. He had mean black eyes and a scar that sliced through his left eyebrow.

She jerked back from the door as though she'd touched an electrified fence. Cody. Fear spiked through her. This man was not Cade's building contractor. This man had shot her father.

CADE STOPPED at the Issaquah police station and talked to his friend in the department. Nothing more had turned up concerning the break-in at Nan's. He hadn't expected anything would have…yet. He asked and received permission for access to her apartment.

Her building, a two-story walk-up, was four blocks west of Front Street. Nancy had moved in the day she'd filed for divorce. It was a one-bedroom with a mini kitchen and a single bathroom. Perfect, she claimed, for a working gal. More of a pit stop between jobs, he thought.

She'd immediately marked her new territory, painted the walls pale yellow, bought baby-blue and floral furniture. Overstuffed and ruffled. It reminded Cade of a little girl's bedroom. In many ways, Nan remained a child. Now that he considered it, both Ted and Nan retained childish facets to their personalities. Their mother had babied and spoiled both of her children without realizing she would one day need them to be responsible adults that she had to rely on.

He gave the room another once-over. He'd visited Nan here on a couple of occasions, but never felt comfortable. Cade had to give Ted credit for one thing, he

conceded begrudgingly: he hadn't exaggerated. Someone had sliced open every cushion, including the backs
and arms of the sofa and overstuffed chair, and Nan's
mattress. A painting, a blurry-edge cityscape, had been
pulled from the wall, the canvas sliced. Lamps were
knocked to the floor, broken, and the contents of every
drawer dumped.

All the classic signs of a search. But a search for
what?

He bent and picked up a sheaf of papers near her
desk. Some receipts. Old case files. Nothing on Cody,
not a birth certificate or anything. Nothing about
Joanna Edwards and her little girl, either. He combed
the clutter one more time looking for Nan's day planner. A calendar. Anything that would give him a clue
where to find her.

Maybe the thieves had it.

Maybe not. "Damn it, Nan. Where are you?"

Why hadn't the blamed woman trusted him enough
to tell him what she'd gotten herself into? Why hadn't
she asked for his help?

Frustrated, he stormed out into the hall. Considering
the damage, someone must have heard something. He
knocked on a couple of Nan's neighbors' doors, but
he learned nothing new. The woman on the left was
hard-of-hearing, the occupant on the right was at work,
and the apartment below hers was vacant.

"Well, that was a waste of time," he grumbled,
stalking back to his car. "Two hours and I still have
no idea where you are, Nan. Don't you care about your
son?"

Feeling as bad for Cody as he was frustrated, Cade
pulled out his cell phone and dialed his home number.
In his haste he failed to notice there was no signal

until he realized the phone wasn't ringing. He needed to get down the freeway and out from the surrounding hills. He pulled onto I-90 moving west toward Seattle. As he reached I-405, he dialed his number again.

This time the call went through. He listened to it ring. And ring. And ring. He shifted lanes, pressing the phone between his ear and his neck as he drove. Where was Joanna? Busy with Cody? He decided to wait five minutes or so and try again.

But five minutes later there was still no answer. Nor five minutes after that. Nor five minutes after that. Fear chattered along his nerve endings and a chill swabbed his spine. Where the hell was she? An awful thought hit him like a punch to the gut.

He'd entrusted his son to a woman who was desperate to find her own baby.

Or any baby?

Her image flashed into his mind. The desperate-eyed woman he'd found sprawled in his kitchen, and later, after she'd been around Cody, the change in her. The desperation gone, replaced by something buoyant, calm, as though she had found a missing piece of herself. With a fear like nothing he'd ever felt, he realized he'd made the biggest mistake of his life leaving Cody with this woman he didn't really know.

Dear God! No! No! No!

Shaking, he snatched the portable flasher from under the seat and slapped it on the roof of his car. Swearing like a madman, he tore through traffic at a high speed.

Still the trip took him a full eight minutes.

He squealed to a stop before his house. Joanna's car was no longer parked down the block. He raced for the front door, key out. His nerves felt raw. He dashed inside. "Joanna?"

He raced from room to room. His hope sank with every passing second. They were nowhere. The house was empty. Her suitcase and purse were gone. The baby's bag was gone. The formula in the refrigerator, gone.

She'd taken his son.

"Mr. Maconahey?"

Cade spun toward the gray-haired man standing in his front door. "Have you seen her?"

The man, dressed in faded coveralls and a paint-splattered baseball cap, blinked and frowned, his snaggly gray eyebrows dipping so low over his eyes as to obscure them. "I beg your pardon?"

"Joanna Edwards. Have you seen her? A blond woman about yeah high—" he gestured with his right hand "—with a baby?"

He shook his head, and wiped at his bulbous nose with a red bandanna. "Well, no. No one was here when I came by earlier."

Cade stopped and stared at the man, realizing he knew him. But his mind was working slow at identifications. The contractor. "Dale Fast."

"Yes. I came by earlier, but nobody answered the door. I guess you forgot about our appointment?"

"I didn't forget." Fast had been due at ten. It was now twelve-thirty. She had a two-, three-hour start. She could have gone anywhere in the world.

Feeling like someone had ripped out his heart, Cade doubled over. Would he ever see his son again? "Cody."

Chapter Six

Dale Fast tapped Cade's arm. "Hey, Mr. Maconahey, you want me to answer your phone?"

The contractor's voice barely penetrated the dull roaring in his brain, in his ears. Cade blinked and tried to focus on the gray-haired man. As though from some long distance or great fog, his senses took hold again, the noise slowly fading. "What?"

"The phone. It's ringing off the hook." Mr. Fast pointed toward the kitchen. "You want me to get it?"

Cade heard it now, the phone, ringing with an insistence that touched the urgency inside him. He shook off the stupor and forced his concrete-clogged legs to move. He plowed through the kitchen and yanked the receiver from the hook. "Maconahey."

"Cade?"

It was Joanna.

He gripped the kitchen counter. His pulse starting to buzz in his ears again. "Where the hell is my son?"

She hesitated, and his fear escalated. Finally her voice came haltingly through the line. "He's here…with me. He's fine. We're both fine."

"You won't get away with this. I'll have every cop in the state after you. I won't quit looking until I find you and bring you back here and see that you're prosecuted.''

She said nothing. The silence echoed through his head like a death sentence handed down by a united jury. Oh, God, he'd blown it. Given in to his temper. His fear. Instead of calmly convincing her to bring Cody home, he'd handed her a fistful of reasons to flee even farther from him.

At length, she said, ''We're at the library...behind your house.''

What? His head jerked up. His gaze flew through the glass door. He dropped the receiver, slammed the door open, tore outside and darted down the path with the speed of a Nascar driver. In seconds, he covered the ground between his house and the library. He stormed through the front doors and up to where she stood by a pay phone.

Catching sight of his son, Cade choked out his name. Cody, perched on Joanna Edwards's hip, plucked at her taffy-blond hair. His face lighted when he spied Cade. Joanna didn't notice him. The diaper bag draped from one of her shoulders. She had the phone at her ear and she kept calling, ''Cade? Cade?''

He grasped her shoulder.

She yelped, rounding on him with a look of sheer terror. But even as she'd turned, she shifted Cody in the opposite direction, away from Cade, her body going protectively around the baby as though she feared he would snatch the boy from her.

Cade reached for his son. Through clenched teeth, he growled, ''Give him to me.''

''Oh, Cade, thank God.'' A breath wobbled out of her. She relinquished Cody and slumped against the phone stall, clutching her arms across her chest forming a huge X. "I was so scared."

Scared? *She* was scared? He held his son against his thundering heart, trying to figure out why and how she could possibly even imagine how terrified he was, let alone be frightened herself. "What the hell is going on?"

"Those men," she blubbered. "Who...this morning. I thought it was the contractor, come early. He said it was. He even knew the right name and that you were expecting him. But it wasn't Dale Fast. One of them was the man who shot my father."

"What?" Cade had expected excuses. A story that made no sense. But he hadn't even considered this. A new kind of fear slid like an oil slick through his stomach. So much for keeping his friends close. He should have rescheduled the contractor and taken Cody and Joanna with him to Issaquah.

"You'd better tell me this again. Slower." He led her to an isolated table in a far corner of the main room. She insisted on sitting with her back to the wall, her view of the library clear. He liked his back to the wall too. He took the chair beside her in order to watch for unwanted company.

He balanced Cody on one thigh. The baby reached for a magazine on the table; Cody loved anything paper. Cade hugged the boy, unable to stop the trembling that had started in him somewhere on the drive home from Issaquah. It was slower, slowing, but still there. "What exactly happened?"

Joanna clutched her hands on the table, wrapped them together like twisted cloth. Her breath was shallow, her face pale, her eyes haunted. "I was doing the laundry. Feeling safe for the first time in a long while.

Safe.'' She shuddered. Ten seconds passed in which she touched Cody's hand, then Cade's, as though reassuring herself they were actually there.

Guilt seared Cade for all the awful things he'd been thinking about this woman. He should have trusted his instincts about her. Should have realized after watching her with Cody that she wouldn't do to anyone what she'd had done to her. She wasn't off her rocker. She wasn't a kidnapper.

She pulled back, her fingers lacing anew. She scanned the room, the library customers. Her shoulders were rigid, her eyes watchful as she verbally walked him through the sequence of events. ''I looked through the peephole. I recognized one of the men.''

Her gaze seemed to glaze over and he knew she was no longer seeing this room, but rather a memory, something dark and personal, something grievous and heinous, something she'd lived through and would like to forget, but would never forget. ''That man shot my father.''

She seemed about to hyperventilate.

''Whoa.'' Cade covered her locked hands with one of his own. ''Take a breath.''

She gave him a grateful look, inhaled deeply, exhaled slowly, then repeated the process twice more. ''Shane sent them for me. I didn't open the door. I told them to hold on a second. That I had to answer the phone. Then I grabbed Cody and climbed out your bedroom window.''

''Why did you first stop at the refrigerator for his formula?''

She arched both eyebrows and color shone high on her cheeks. ''I did no such thing.''

''The formula's gone.''

"I used the last of it this morning. I thought we'd get more this afternoon."

Cade's guilt thickened. He'd leaped to some lousy conclusions. But, hell, the evidence... "Your car is gone."

"My car?" She frowned, not seeming to understand, as though this was one thing too many to take in after all she'd been through today. "My car is gone?"

"Did you go back for it?"

"God, no." She sat straighter, shaking her head. "I wouldn't have risked that. I came over here and stayed in the library. There were people here. Witnesses. Safety in numbers. I didn't dare go back. Not for anything."

"Then where is your car?"

"How should I know?"

He leaned toward her. "Could Addison's thugs have taken it?"

"Not without the key." She wrinkled her nose in distaste and her gaze swept the room again. "It won't start unless the alarm is disengaged. They couldn't do that unless they somehow popped the trunk. And even then, for a while, until it was deactivated, the alarm would've roused your neighbors' curiosity."

He thought about that a moment as Cody tugged the magazine closer and scratched his nails on its clear, hard plastic jacket. "Could they have gotten the key?"

"The only key is in my purse, in your guest room." Her eyes widened, the green so dark they seemed obsidian. "Oh, my God, did they break into the house and steal my keys?"

Cade saw again the guest room as he'd found it

minutes earlier. Neither her purse nor her suitcase had been there. It was one of the reasons he'd thought she'd run off.

"The house wasn't broken into." He shook his head.

"Are you sure?"

"Fairly sure." He wrested the magazine from Cody inches short of the pages landing in the baby's mouth. Cody let out an unhappy squeal and stretched his tiny arms again for the periodical. "The front door was still locked when I arrived home."

"And the glass door?"

"Locked." He handed Cody his keys to play with, but then took them away as he realized Cody was about to shove them into his mouth.

"Oh, God, the window." She smacked herself in the forehead with the heel of her hand. "I didn't stop to close it when we fled."

Cade stood and adjusted Cody to his shoulder. He reached a hand for her. "Let's go back. I want to take another look around my little castle."

"No way. I'm not going back there."

"We have to. I need to call the Auburn police."

"But those men might still be lurking nearby. Watching."

"Then that's another reason to get back—because I left the real Dale Fast standing in the living room with both the front and glass doors hanging open. He's probably thinking he's been hired by a lunatic."

Her gaze searched the library customers another time, then returned to him. She nodded, rising, reluctance in the set of her shoulders, the angle of her jaw. He guessed she'd rather run than go back to his house.

HE ACTUALLY THOUGHT I'd run off with Cody. The realization had robbed Joanna of the warmth his earlier
trust had given her. She'd considered setting him
straight, telling him that she would never steal another's child after having her own stolen. She understood too well the devastation that wrought. But knowing one day that she would both steal his child and
break his heart, she'd held her tongue.

Now, however, as they hurried to his house, she
wrestled a stomach full of guilt. Cade held the baby
so close she could see he was terrified of losing him.
She hated that he felt this possessive, but she understood it with every ounce of her being. And somehow
with the baby tucked in Cade's strong embrace she
felt Cody was more protected.

She ached to feel that same sense of protection, of
love. Would she ever? Would she ever trust another
man as she'd trusted Adam Shane? Would she ever
again walk through this world without looking over
her shoulder? Without fearing that someone would
take her child from her?

She had to admit she did feel less afraid, buoyed
even, having this strapping man at her side. But he
would soon hate her. Forever hate her. She longed to
end this charade. She didn't want to hurt Cade as she'd
been hurt, as he would be hurt, but she had no choice.
This morning had shown her that.

She quickened her pace and shoved away the worry
over claiming Cody. She needed to deal with the present, not the future. *Had* Shane's hitmen stolen her car?
Anger warmed her blood. If so, why? Just because
they could? Just to show her nothing of hers was sacred? Hell, they'd already shown her that by murdering her father. So, what other reason could they have

had? Maybe to search it—as Nancy's apartment had been searched?

All to find and destroy her baby.

More than ever she knew she mustn't do anything to give away that Cody was *her* son. The world and Cade Maconahey had to go on thinking Cody was *his* son. Above all else, Cody had to be and was her main concern. So, despite how much she regretted the heartache this would cause Cade, she would do whatever it took to keep Cody safe.

As they entered the sliding glass door, Cade said, "Let me put this little guy down for his nap, then I'll get the local boys in blue looking for your car."

A noise from the back hall startled them both. He touched a finger to his lips and made a silent signal for her to stay where she was. He handed Cody to her, crept into the hall and retrieved his Glock from the top shelf of the linen closet. He disengaged the safety, then, leading with the gun, he tiptoed to the point of the noise: the guest bedroom.

A soft whistling froze him in his tracks. A happy intruder? Warily, he poked his head around the corner. Dale Fast was stretching his measuring tape from one end of the room to the other, then writing on a tablet.

He glanced up when he saw Cade. "Ah, Mr. Maconahey. You've come back. I hope you don't mind. I thought I might as well get this done so I can work up your bid."

The contractor's gaze fell on the gun and he stepped back, startled. "Is something wrong?"

"No. Sorry." Chagrined, Cade lowered the gun, thumbing on the safety. "Glad you stayed, Mr. Fast."

He spoke this last loud enough for Joanna to hear from the kitchen.

Dale Fast's shaggy gray eyebrows lifted. "You find the woman and the baby?"

If the contractor thought his earlier behavior odd, or his behavior now, he showed no sign of it. "Yes."

"Good. I'll be finished here in a minute."

Fast had the closet door open and Cade could see it was empty. He scanned the room. No, he hadn't been wrong. Joanna's suitcase and purse were gone. In fact, he'd swear all trace of her had been removed from his guest room as though she'd never been here. What the hell?

Nan's apartment flashed into his mind, the deliberate damage and destruction. He was struck by the complete contrast of this tidy dismissal of Joanna Edwards that he saw before him.

Who were these guys? What was this game?

Cade left Fast to his measuring. He'd already compromised the crime scene, added his prints to any the thieves might have deposited here. Cade put the Glock away and headed toward his bedroom. He wanted a look at that open window and the ground beneath it. Not that he expected to find much. Since Cody's arrival, he hadn't watered any of the flower beds. If he didn't do it soon he might lose all of his roses.

As he approached the open window, he thought again about the intruders stealing Joanna's purse and her clothes as well as her car. Why? If all the perps had wanted was to search her belongings, it seemed most likely they'd have done it here.

Cade had a bad feeling in his gut about this.

THE SEARING PANIC in Joanna's gut fled as she heard Cade call the intruder "Mr. Fast." The contractor. Her breath quavered out of her and she closed and locked the glass door.

"We should have realized it would be Dale Fast," she told Cody, moving away from the door where she'd been perched ready for flight, if necessary. "After all, Cade did mention he'd left the poor man standing in the living room when he ran to the library to find us."

The baby chattered in answer, a gibberish slew of words, his expression as earnest as though he understood and concurred.

Joanna grinned and hugged him close. "You are the most precious thing."

Cody shoved against her hold. She lifted him away from her so she could see his face more clearly. "I'll bet you're sick and tired of being held as if you were in restraints, huh?"

He squealed with distress and stretched his arm toward the table. She glanced in the direction of his interest. The baby-food jars. She hadn't had time, or any idea of where, to put them away yet. "Oh, so that's it. Well, I think we can take care of what ails you, young man."

She chose carrots from the stack of jars, found a clean bib and dish towel and settled into the kitchen chair with her son on her lap. Her chin brushed his downy blond hair and filled her with a heated joy and a cruel nip of anger. This was one of the simple pleasures Nancy Wheeler had denied her.

Joanna bit down her ire. How could she waste even one minute of the cherished time she now had with her son dwelling on that which she'd lost and could never retrieve? No. She would not do that.

She kissed the top of his head, then fed him

spoonful of strained carrots. Cody gobbled it up, his mouth falling open for the next bite. Orange goo rimmed his tiny mouth. The sight warmed her from the inside out, exploding in a smile. It felt so good to hold him, relaxed, without worry that someone was bearing down on them.

But how safe were they here...now that Shane knew her whereabouts?

Cade clambered into the kitchen, his expression shadowed, dark. The nerves in her stomach revived. "What's wrong?"

"Besides someone breaking into my house and stealing your car?" He sounded flippant, but there was no mistaking the ferocious set of his jaw, the taut lines around his appealing mouth.

His gaze fell on Cody and the steel in his blue eyes softened. He strode toward them and touched the baby's head with two fingers, a gesture full of love. Her heart twisted with guilt. Cody ignored Cade. He was only interested in his food.

Cade lifted his gaze to her. "The sooner there's a BOLB on your car, the better."

She arched an eyebrow at him. "A BOLB?"

"Be on the lookout bulletin."

She nodded. "What aren't you telling me?"

Cade pressed his lips together. "The intruders...did come in through the window. I'm going to have the place dusted for prints."

"And...?"

He blew out a noisy breath. "And...along with your car, they took your purse and your luggage."

"What!" Joanna jerked as though he'd poked her. She cursed under her breath and shook her head, hard.

"Why would they do that? Steal my clothes? My personal items—"

She broke off, her eyes narrowing. "Oh, I know. To make me feel vulnerable. As though I've been violated. Well, the hell with that. I won't be intimidated by Shane Addison or his henchmen."

Cody shoved his fingers into the carrot jar, shrieked with delight and began flapping his hand, flinging specks of carrot everywhere. Despite her fury, Joanna laughed and snatched for the towel, struggling to catch the tiny hand. "You little stinker. You're as effective as a sprinkler."

CADE WATCHED her tender machinations with his son. Despite the turmoil and fury she had to be feeling, despite the fact that she now had carroty goop splattering her face, her hair and her only remaining clothes, she was gentle with his baby. Joanna Edwards deserved better than life had been giving her. If there was some way for him to even out the scales, he damn well would.

"I'd better clean us up," she said. Giving Cade a bemused grin, she carried Cody from the room.

Cade spun toward the wall phone. The receiver was still on the floor where he'd dropped it. Static emitted from the earpiece. He jammed the disconnect button with his finger. Before he could lift it, the phone rang.

He reared back, startled. Then, grinning at himself, he answered, "Maconahey."

"Cade?" It was Ted, and he sounded as upset as Cade felt.

Had he heard from Nan?

Cade held his breath, praying that he had, that something on this wretched day would finally go for them instead of against them. He strove to hide his rising hope, knowing if he sounded calm he might get his ex-brother-in-law to calm down, too. "What's going on, Ted?"

"It's Nan."

Cade's pulse danced. "She contacted you, right?"

"How'd you know? She called me earlier. This morning. I...arranged to meet her...for coffee."

"Damn it, Ted." Fury shot through Cade. "Why didn't you call me?"

"She made me promise not to."

Cade swore again. "Where is she?"

"She was supposed to meet me at SouthCenter. At the mall." His voice was an annoying whine. "She didn't come. I waited two hours and she didn't come."

Frustration washed through Cade, rousing every bitter feeling he'd harbored for his ex-wife since she'd dropped Cody off last week. Damn the woman. Who knew where she was now? "I thought we had a deal, Ted. What if I'd pulled this on you?"

"You don't understand, Cade."

"Save your excuses. There's nothing you can say right now that's going to make this up to me."

"I know where she is."

"What? Where?"

"The police came...half an hour ago."

"The police? What police?" Cade's stomach clenched. "What are you saying?"

"They received an anonymous tip. When they investigated, they found Nan...at the mall. In the parking lot. She was in the trunk of a car."

The words rang loud and strident inside Cade's head, filling him with dread. "Is she—?"

"Dead?" Ted sobbed. "Yes."

Cade swore. "How?"

"Stabbed...with an ordinary kitchen knife."

"Oh, God, no. No!" Cade closed his eyes and said a silent prayer for the woman he had once loved, the mother of his son. "Who did this to her, Ted? Do the police have any idea?"

"Yes. They think it was the woman whose car she was found in. They're looking for her now. A Joanna Edwards from Spokane."

Chapter Seven

Cade hung up the phone, but couldn't seem to release it, as if letting go would be to admit Nancy was dead. Murdered. Found in Joanna's stolen car. He felt numb, stunned, sick.

"Mr. Maconahey, I'm all done measuring. I'll just work up my figures and have you a bid—" Dale Fast broke off. "Is something wrong, sir? You're as white as taping mud."

Cade lifted his gaze to the contractor. "Bad news."

"I'm sorry." Mr. Fast looked ill at ease, obviously uncomfortable with anything that didn't concern business.

"Thank you," Cade said. He ushered the contractor to the door. "I may be gone for a day or two. Why don't you mail me that bid and I'll get back to you shortly afterward?"

"Sure."

Cade closed the front door and slumped against it. He slammed his hands through his hair and swore. "Oh, God, Nan. Why didn't you trust me?"

Cody. Oh, Cody. How would he ever explain this to his son? The thought of that precious little boy growing up never knowing his mother widened the crack in Cade's heart. He knew *that* pain too well, the pain of abandonment and loss.

Joanna. Her face, full of happiness and joy as she interacted with his son, flashed through his mind's eye. What about her child now, her little girl? He groaned. Good God in heaven, how was he going to tell her that the only person who knew where her baby was had been murdered and *she* was the prime suspect?

He sank to his haunches, his arms wrapped around his aching gut, his gaze riveted on the dust motes floating through a band of sunlight that angled across the coffee table. The room was warm, but he felt cold, cold to the bone, cold to his soul.

His brain screamed for action; he couldn't move. He was a licensed police officer. He had one clear path. Call the Tukwila department and tell them their chief suspect was here. In his house. Not to do that was to commit a crime, to harbor a criminal.

With every ounce of his being, Cade was an honest cop. A good cop. Nan was the first person he'd ever trusted enough to love. Even then he'd held back on her. Hadn't totally given his heart. That, more than his job, more than her kookiness, had been at the root of their breakup.

They were mismatched. Had little or nothing in common, except between the sheets. It was the one area where they were compatible. The only one. In many ways she'd never grown up, whereas he'd grown up too fast too young. They were the consummate opposites. She was optimistic and trusting. He was rebellious, antisocial, cynical.

Maybe that explained why she hadn't told him what trouble she'd gotten into. A spark of ire flared in his belly, the small flame quickly combusting into a white-hot rage. He wanted the devils who'd done this. Wanted them so badly he could taste it.

But how? No way he would be let in on this investigation. Not with his past and present relationship to Nan. Not with his new relationship to Joanna. He doubted the detectives in charge would hear suggestions that the leading candidate for governor might be involved at the highest levels. "Damn. Damn. Damn."

What would he do if he were in charge? Cade rocked back on his heels, forcing the grief aside, calling on the objectivity he practiced on a regular basis in his work. First, what about Joanna? According to the facts as he knew them, could she have killed Nan?

He glanced at the clock. He'd left around nine and returned at twelve-thirty. She'd phoned at, say, twelve thirty-five. So, that was three hours. Could she prove she was at the library the whole time? He supposed the librarians might have noticed her. He made a mental note to find out.

Could she have lied about the intruders? He'd discovered dirt on his bedroom windowsill that wouldn't have gotten there by someone exiting from inside. There was a scuff mark made, it appeared, by a dark shoe. Joanna wore sandals.

But suppose she had wanted him to believe there were intruders? She would have planted these clues. If she'd done that, then what might have happened? He narrowed his eyes trying to imagine a scenario that fit the facts, such as Nancy showing up here, refusing to tell Joanna who had her baby, and trying, perhaps, to take Cody from her.

So, Joanna had what? Gone berserk and stabbed Nancy with, say, one of his kitchen knives? She'd then driven her car to the backyard, somehow managed to carry and wrestle the unwieldy dead body into the trunk in broad daylight without any of his nosy neighbors noticing?

Then she'd packed up her suitcase and purse, leaving both in the car so that she'd be sure to be identified, just in case her fingerprints all over the car interior, not to mention the car's license and registration, wouldn't lead the police to her?

Was he expected to believe she was this stupid and that she'd done all of this with Cody in tow, and managed somehow to get back here to the library without a vehicle? Without a change of clothes, without a speck of blood on her?

No. It was impossible. She hadn't killed Nan. He knew that in his gut, the way he knew Mrs. Lei, the grandmother with the innocent Asian face, was the brains behind the white slave trading racket he'd helped break up last month. His hunch had paid off. His hunches usually did. He listened to his gut. Right now, his gut was screaming Joanna's innocence.

He rose. Blew breath out his nostrils. Granted, she had the best, most obvious motive. Hell, even he had motive. He paced the room, rubbing his hands across his head. Cody was his motive. He'd already filed for full custody. A case could likely be made that no judge would award an unmarried, undercover vice cop full custody of a child that he would seldom see.

Fury swept him again and he paced faster, clenching and unclenching his hands, slamming a fist into his palm. Swearing. "Damn. Damn. Damn."

Joanna intruded on his private tirade. "I've got Cody down for his nap, and I managed to wash most of the carrot off my clothes."

Cade pivoted and stared at her. She had wet spots

all over her T-shirt and jeans. Her tawny hair was freshly combed and fell in wavy radiance around her pretty face. She wrung her hands in front of her, the only outward sign of her anxiousness over the theft of her personal items and her clothes.

God, he dreaded shattering the fragile hold she had on her poise.

She studied his face, reading him in that instant. "Has something more happened? What is it?"

Cade pressed his lips together, holding in the awful news. One of the things he enjoyed about working undercover was that he never had to inform anyone about a death. He couldn't deal with the victims' families' shock or grief. Now he was the one suffering shock and grief. And more.

"Cade, you're scaring me. Tell me." Joanna moved toward him.

He motioned to the sofa. She frowned, nodded, walked woodenly to his leather couch and sat on the edge. He sank beside her, leaning his forearms on his thighs, burying his face in his hands. Such nice hands, she noticed. Big, strong hands that held Cody with a tenderness and protectiveness she envied. Would those hands also be gentle hands on a woman? she wondered, wanting to concentrate on anything but the bad news she was certain he had to share.

This day had already been hell. She couldn't imagine, didn't want to imagine, what could be worse. He shook his head, and her concern tripled. She lifted her hand to touch his shoulder, instinctively knowing that he needed comforting. "Can you tell me?"

He raised his head, looked at her and nodded. "That was Ted on the phone. Nan's dead."

Joanna gasped. "No. How? What happened?"

Cade told her, leaving nothing out.

As she listened, she began to tremble. "Why Nancy?"

"All I can think is that they wanted to find your baby and she wouldn't tell them."

"My baby..." Joanna covered her mouth, feeling sick. Because of her, people were dying. "We have to call the police. Tell them about the intruders, tell them about my car being stolen."

She started to rise. He caught her arm gently, pulling her back down, holding her. He shook his head. "Not a good idea. I would have agreed with you if I'd been able to report the car stolen before Nan's body was found. But now, now it would look like we were covering up."

"Covering up what? Nancy's murder?"

He caught her hands in his. "The police are looking for you. They want to question you. But I suspect they'll arrest you if we show up at the station."

"Jail?" She blinked and swallowed hard. Her eyes flew wide open. "But I'm innocent. I didn't do it. I haven't seen Nancy Wheeler for seven months."

"I believe you."

She looked surprised. "Do you?"

Her words were an accusation. He released her hands and rubbed his jaw, silently cursing himself. She had every right to be suspicious, taken aback at his quick capitulation. In a matter of an hour or so, he'd gone from believing her guilty of kidnapping, to believing her innocent of murder—all without a blink.

He wouldn't blame her if she threatened to walk out on Cody and him. Not that he would allow that now; she was in way more trouble and danger than she knew. Before he told her that, he needed to make her understand his commitment to her was serious. "Would I be risking my job if I didn't believe you?"

"Risking?" She shook her head. "No. You mustn't. I can't let you do that."

"I guess you'd rather spend your life in prison? Or risk hanging?" He made no effort to soften his tone or his words. He meant to scare her, but she was way ahead of him.

"I can't go to jail. He'll have me killed." Her voice shook, but her chin was jutted high. Addison hadn't broken her spirit. Or her determination. She blew out a quavery breath. "Oh, it will look like an accident, but it won't be one. You know I'm right."

"I know." Such things did happen to inmates. It would happen to Joanna. He would stake his career on it. He *was* staking his career on it. Shane Addison had silenced Lonnie Edwards and Nan. He was coming after Joanna now with a vengeance. If the police didn't get her, his hired guns would.

"I can't involve you and Cody. I have to get out of here."

"How? You don't even have a car now."

"I'll call a friend. She'll come and get me."

"I can't let you do that."

"Try and stop me."

He caught her arm once again, halting her rise from the couch. "Do you want to put your friend in jeopardy?"

"I'm putting you and Cody in jeopardy. Those men this morning knew your contractor's name, the time he was expected. Your house is probably bugged."

Cade laughed derisively. "There's no need for bugs these days. Not with the laser technology that's available. All someone has to do is sit in their car outside to hear everything we're saying, the sound quality so clear it's like they were standing in the room with us. Hell, there's equipment that allows someone to see you move from room to room. Hear you breathe while you sleep.''

She shuddered and a dawning light of horror filled her eyes. ''So, that's how they knew which route Dad and I were taking to the church. And where I was headed this time.''

''Yeah. Probably.''

Her emerald eyes darkened with pain and guilt, but anger glowed in their very depths. She looked to him like other victims he'd encountered whose privacy had been violated in one way or another. Like those victims, a part of her seemed to feel she'd brought this on herself. ''I thought I'd been so careful, only telling my best girlfriend where I was going, never realizing we were being overheard. I never meant to bring this trouble on you.''

''When Addison ordered Nan's death, he plunked me smack into the middle of this. Not you. I won't let him get away it. Nan didn't deserve to die like she did. Addison isn't going to kill you, too.''

''But Cody—''

''Has lost his mother.'' Fury burned Cade's belly. ''Addison is going to pay for that.''

''How? I…we…'' A look of sheer hopelessness filled her eyes. Then tears. She swiped at them, her lips, those luscious lips puckering with anger, fighting, he suspected, to hold back a flood.

He reached out and gathered her into his arms. She melded against him with the ease of a ship gliding into its slip. Her arms stole around his waist, mooring lines lashing her to him, as though he were her anchor.

Her back trembled beneath his hands as she sobbed into his chest. Cade had no idea why she touched him as she did, but he had no qualms about breaking the law in order to save this woman's life, and hopefully, one day, someway, he would reunite her with her daughter.

Her tears subsided into a quiet mewling, and she lifted her head, wiping her cheeks with the heels of her hands. She didn't apologize, wasn't concerned with the mascara smeared around her eyes. "We can't stay here. We have to think of Cody. Have to keep him out of this. Safe."

"Safe." Cade swore. He glanced at the clock on the mantel and swore again. "Unless I miss my guess, we don't have much time. Addison's people seem bent on framing you. They know you're here. Very likely the Tukwila police have already gotten another anonymous tip telling them that. We've gotta leave. Now."

They both leaped to their feet. Cade tossed her the keys to his SUV. "You grab some clean baby clothes and load a sack with baby food. I'll get Cody and the diaper bag. We'll pick up some formula on the way."

Cade ran to the linen closet and retrieved his Glock, strapped on his shoulder holster and grabbed a couple of extra clips, which he stuffed into the bottom of the diaper bag. Despite the heat, he donned a lightweight sports jacket. Too aware of the time slipping away, he hastened toward the bed. Cody was still asleep, but one whiff of the air told Cade they wouldn't be going anywhere until he had a fresh diaper. He groaned and lifted the cardboard barrier from the bed. "You've got lousy timing, son."

How much time did they have? Joanna worried as she yanked paper sacks from under the sink. She tugged clothes from the dryer and stuffed them into one of the bags, then filled the other with baby-food jars and a box of rice cereal. Terror made her jumpy, her movements jerky. She gathered the two sacks against her thundering heart and hurried into the hallway.

She shouted to Cade, "Do you need any help?"

"No. We'll be right there—as soon as I change Cody."

"Okay, I'll meet you in the SUV."

She raced out to his SUV with the sacks, opened the back door and scrambled in on her knees. She tucked the sacks into the space behind the back seat. The sound of tires squealing brought her jerking around. She peered out the windshield. Coming down the road were six cars, the first four were dark blue, almost black, bearing the insignia of the Tukwila police.

Joanna's breath clogged her throat. She eased the door shut and ducked down on the floorboards. Her heart galloped against her ribs. She prayed the cops had been so intent on spotting Cade's house none of them had seen her through the darkly tinted SUV windows.

If she was wrong, she was dead.

Chapter Eight

Cade stripped the offending diaper off Cody, then fought to keep the baby on his back until he could clean his bottom and put on the fresh diaper. Anxiety made him more clumsy than usual at the task. He tried to gently lift the tabs as Joanna had shown him, but in his haste, he once again tore them from the diaper.

Silently cursing himself, he grabbed the duct tape and ripped off two strips. Getting Cody back into his clothes was like dressing a squirming wildcat. The baby jabbered gleefully as though he was being most cooperative. Cade laughed and lifted him. "Come on, little guy. We've got a lady waiting on us."

He lifted the car seat from beside the bed and strapped Cody into it.

Precious time was being wasted. He hurried to the front door. Joanna had left it open. To his horror, a swarm of cars was pulling to a stop outside. Cade froze. His heart clenched. He hovered in the doorway, hoisting the baby carrier higher onto his forearm.

His gaze shot to the SUV in time to see the back door shut. Joanna. "Good Lord."

There were four dark blue Tukwila patrol cars and two unmarked sedans. Men ran from the vehicles en masse. There were several uniforms and two suits. A command staff.

Cade took a bracing breath and forced the stress from his expression. Praying none of the officers would glance inside his SUV, he drew their attention by standing like a barrier in the door frame, as though he had something to hide inside the house.

He thanked God he'd had the SUV windows tinted the darkest shade available. "What's going on, guys?"

One of the uniformed officers approached him. "Cade Maconahey?"

"That's right."

The other uniforms disappeared around the sides of his house. Cade knew what they were doing. Knew why they were here. He pretended he didn't. "What's wrong?"

The uniform eyed the doorway, trying to see beyond Cade. The officer stood about five feet away, talking loudly, hoping to draw Cade outside, away from the door. He said, "We're with the Tukwila police. I'm Officer O'Brien. This is Detective Tollard."

O'Brien might be a middleweight champion boxer, big and brown and bald, his body lithe, agile. His eyes, hard chips of slate, missed nothing. He had the air of a man who paid attention to detail, personally and professionally. His hand rested on the butt of the gun strapped to his waist.

Detective Tollard was his opposite. He was too thin, too white and too hairy. He looked as if he lived on coffee, cigarettes and nerves. His skin had the pallor of a computer jockey. A shaggy salt-and-pepper mustache rode his upper lip. He'd nicked his chin shaving that morning, and hadn't bothered wiping off the speck of dried blood marking the spot.

Tollard said, "Could I speak with you over here, Mr. Maconahey?"

"I'm a Seattle police detective," Cade informed them, adding that he was just reaching for his shield. He pulled it from his jacket pocket and showed it to O'Brien and Tollard.

Immediately the level of courtesy rose. "I'm sorry, sir, we weren't told." O'Brien's hand came off his gun.

"Why are you here?" Cade hadn't budged from the door.

Tollard gestured for Cade to join him on the lawn, near the sidewalk. Cade wanted to keep their attention focused on the house and not on the SUV. The best way to do that was to let them think there was something—or someone—to find in the house.

He pulled the door closed behind him and moved to where Tollard stood. He knew closing the door upped their suspicion. It was a calculated move. He was whetting their appetites, urging to a frenzy their eagerness to search the house.

O'Brien took up a stance beside the door, but he made no move to go inside. He dare not, not without consent or a warrant.

Tollard said, "We're looking for Joanna Edwards, the woman in whose car your ex-wife's body was discovered this morning. We received a call from someone a while ago who said we could find her here."

Cade frowned and shook his head. "Well, your tipster is wrong. Ted Wheeler told me your prime suspect is this Edwards woman. Believe me, I want whoever killed Nan as badly as you. I wouldn't be harboring her murderer."

"And I believe you." Tollard stroked his mustache. "But I'd like you to sign a consent-of-search form."

"What?" Cade grimaced. This would take at least forty-five minutes to an hour. Joanna could suffocate in the SUV in that time. "You want to search my house?"

"Routine. You know that. Is it a problem?"

Cade could see no way out of this. If he didn't allow a search, he'd seem guilty of something, as guilty as he was and felt. He hated lying to this man. Hated going against everything he believed in. But sometimes bending the rules was the only means of survival, the only way to achieve justice. "I was on my way to get some baby formula. I'm out."

"A friend of Ms. Edwards confirmed she was coming to see you," Tollard said.

"I can't account for what she told her friend. I haven't seen the woman."

Tollard studied his face, smoothing his mustache. "Ted Wheeler told us you had a blond woman fitting Ms. Edwards's description here the other night."

Cade shook his head. *Typical Ted,* he thought, glad that he'd introduced Joanna to his ex-brother-in-law by a false name. "My brother-in-law is an idiot. If you met him, you already know that. The woman he mentioned was Ellen Donahue, a friend of a friend. I was thinking of hiring her to help out with my son. But Cody didn't take to her and she left an hour after Ted."

"I see. So, what about that consent-to-search form? Will you sign it?"

Cade's pulse hammered his temples. "I've got nothing to hide. I'm just concerned about the time it will take. I really need to pick up some formula for my son.''

Tollard promised they'd make it quick. Quick was forty-five minutes; each second passed like a lifetime for Cade. His mind filled with images of Joanna, slowly succumbing to the heat inside the SUV. He wrestled against the visions while he tried getting Tollard to give him details about Nan's murder.

The detective wasn't in a sharing mood. He wanted to ask questions not answer them, starting with, ''Joanna Edwards's friend also claims Nancy Wheeler ran off with the Edwards woman's baby daughter. You know anything about that?''

''No.'' Cade returned Tollard's curious stare with a hard one of his own. ''Nan and I never discussed her business.''

''Why is that?''

''We were divorced.''

''For five years, I hear.'' Tollard glanced at Cody, who was sucking on his pacifier, his eyes closed, his lashes long and dark against his chubby cheeks. ''Nice-looking kid, is his mother around?''

''You're investigating his mother's murder.''

''You and Nancy Wheeler had a kid together?''

Cade scowled at the man. ''We were divorced. We weren't enemies.''

Tollard raised his eyebrows suggestively and glanced away. Toward the SUV. Cade wanted to hit the man, wanted to unleash his tension on him. With an effort, he restrained himself. ''Now you know why I want her killer caught.''

Tollard looked back at Cody, then at Cade, taking his anger as a reaction to Nan's murder. He nodded and switched the subject to the Seahawks, then the Mariners.

Cade moved the baby carrier from side to side, a gentle rocking motion that soothed Cody. He wished for something to soothe his own tattered nerves. It took every ounce of will he possessed not to glance at the SUV, not to march over to it and open all the windows, not to show the anxiety he felt over Joanna in that oppressively hot vehicle.

When it seemed the nightmare would never end, the officers emerged from his house, reported finding nothing to indicate Ms. Edwards had ever been there, thanked Cade for his cooperation, apologized for the inconvenience and started toward their cars.

To his horror, instead of getting into his car, O'Brien was eyeing the SUV curiously.

With his heart in his throat, Cade forced himself to turn away and walk to his front door.

JOANNA LAY HUNCHED against the floorboards, every muscle in her body clenched and stiff. Sweat drenched her hair, trickled between her breasts, dampened her underarms and pasted her T-shirt and jeans to her. Her head thumped and the smell of the rubber mat made her nauseous.

There was a sudden swelling of male voices from outside the SUV. Fresh talons of fear dug into her. A roaring filled her ears, eclipsing all other sound. She might have gone deaf. Bile burned the back of her throat. The front door of the SUV was wrenched open. Terror froze her brain. Her tongue. She was dead.

"Joanna?"

She shivered, huddling in on herself. The back door opened.

Her heart stopped. Air, fresh and cooler than that inside the vehicle, filtered to her nostrils. She inhaled sharply and it revived her. "Joanna!"

Cade. It was Cade's voice. Oh, God, thank you. She struggled to unbend her cramped legs and arms. It had been like being locked in a heat box. The prolonged lack of fresh oxygen had made her woozy. With his help, she managed to rise and sink onto the back seat. He had placed Cody on the front seat, she saw, and had left both doors on the driver's side hanging open.

Cade slid in next to her and handed her a container of bottled water. "Drink. Slowly."

She took a sip, stifling the urge to gulp. The liquid was cool and wet and refreshing. Reviving. She took deep breaths, and the pounding at her temples elevated.

Cade asked, "Are you okay?"

"My head aches like hell, but some aspirin should take care of that." A temblor vibrated deep within her body. She tried giving him a brave smile but only half succeeded. What this man had risked—was risking—for her was incredible. She wanted to thank him, but her throat was parched. He made her take another sip of water. She felt stronger with every swallow.

He smoothed a strand of sticky hair from her face, his touch gentle and sensuous. She knew she was a sight, her hair smashed to her head, her mascara smeared, her lip gloss gone. He seemed not to notice. His eyes shone with a heated yearning, a desire that was less sexual and more emotional, as though he sought something he sensed he'd find in her.

Her heart tugged and something she could neither name nor explain, something deep within, rose and reached out to his need, silently, spiritually speaking a language without words. He lowered his mouth to hers, a quick brush across her lips, a physical connection to test the emotional one he sought. Her toes curled and a different warmth swept through her and eased her throbbing head.

Cody began to fuss. Cade gave Joanna a discomfited smile. "We'd better get him some formula. Are you going to be okay back here?"

"Yes." As he stowed a duffel bag in the back next to Cody's things, she fastened her seat belt and settled into the seat, wishing she could stretch out on it instead as exhaustion suddenly laid claim to her. She'd had a hell of a day. A long nap sounded wonderful.

Cade started the engine and turned on the air-conditioning. "First stop, Smart-Mart."

As they left his neighborhood, they passed a white van with KIMI Channel 3 News emblazoned on its side turning onto his street.

Cade swore. "The vultures have picked up the scent."

But neither police nor media, Cade made sure, were following them. At Smart-Mart, he left Joanna in the car with Cody, and bought formula, a convertible travel bed/playpen, a backpack baby carrier and more diapers, a couple of changes of clothing, makeup and toiletries for Joanna and shaving essentials for himself.

WHILE CADE SHOPPED, Joanna spent the time alternating between ducking and hiding her face, as jumpy as she'd been earlier. She had no illusions that by now her image was plastered all over the news. She was being sought by the police. At any moment someone might recognize her.

She was relieved when he finally returned, glad too

that night was falling. In it she felt she could disappear, become anonymous, at least for a while. They stowed the new purchases in the back of the SUV, strapped Cody's car seat into the back seat and climbed into the front.

"I don't know about you, but I'm starving," Cade said.

"Ah, food. That sounds wonderful."

"Any particular preference?"

"Hot and quick."

Cade selected a fast-food restaurant, used the drive-through and ordered cheeseburgers, fries and sodas. Joanna chewed her hamburger, discovering she was ravenous. She glanced back at Cody. He was sucking on a French fry, making a mess of his car seat. The joy of even that warmed her heart. She touched his cheek, fear for him still frazzling the edges of her nerves. They had to find a way to end this war with Shane, to ensure this child's safety. "Where are we going?"

Cade glanced at her, his face in shadow. "I've got a friend who won't mind if we borrow her cabin on Lake Retreat."

"Is that far from here?"

"No. It's out past Four Corners and Ravensdale, about half an hour at most."

They rode in silence, eating. Cade seemed relaxed, but Joanna noticed he constantly checked the rearview mirror. Did he think someone was following them? *Was* someone following them? Her muscles tensed. Would Cade continue to his friend's cabin if he thought so?

She offered Cody another French fry, peering out the back window. All she saw were headlights. To her, they all looked the same. If someone was following them, she couldn't tell.

Soon the signs of civilization gave way to tall firs and two-lane roads. Darkness closed in on them, and the traffic behind dropped off to one or two vehicles. Cade seemed less edgy. Cody was contentedly gumming another fry. Joanna allowed herself to breathe easy for the first time all day.

Anyone looking at them might think they were seeing a common, contented family outing, a Norman Rockwell painting. Was this what she thought she'd have when she fell in love with Adam Shane in Paris? When she'd agreed to marry Bob? Or did she know what she wanted? Had she ever known? Ever been allowed to figure that out for herself? It seemed she'd been spinning out of control, never taking charge, letting others make her life choices.

The few times she'd stabbed out on her own, fate had changed her options, and she'd invariably given in to emotion instead of taking charge. This time, Shane was controlling her destiny, her future, the future of her child. She had to stand up to him, to stop him, take back her life. "What are we going to do, Cade?"

"I guess we've got all night to figure that out." He drove through a privacy hedge and onto a graveled parking area. A vapor light, perched high on a pole, shone yellow on a two-story cabin, shaped, as far as Joanna could tell in the limited light, like two shoe boxes stacked one atop the other. A railed porch seemed to run the length of the building on the side that faced the lake.

Like a mirror laid in the center of an elfin village, the lake reflected the waxing moon and myriad stars

he Harlequin Reader Service® — Here's how it works:

epting your 2 free books and gift places you under no obligation to buy anything. You may keep the books and gift
return the shipping statement marked "cancel." If you do not cancel, about a month later we'll send you 4 additional
els and bill you just $3.57 each in the U.S., or $3.96 each in Canada, plus 25¢ shipping & handling per book and
licable taxes if any.* That's the complete price and — compared to cover prices of $4.25 each in the U.S. and $4.99
n in Canada — it's quite a bargain! You may cancel at any time, but if you choose to continue, every month we'll send
4 more books, which you may either purchase at the discount price or return to us and cancel your subscription.

rms and prices subject to change without notice. Sales tax applicable in N.Y. Canadian residents will be charged
licable provincial taxes and GST.

If offer card is missing write to: Harlequin Reader Service, 3010 Walden Ave., P.O. Box 1867, Buffalo NY 14240-1867

NO POSTAGE
NECESSARY
IF MAILED
IN THE
UNITED STATES

BUSINESS REPLY MAIL

FIRST-CLASS MAIL   PERMIT NO. 717   BUFFALO, NY

POSTAGE WILL BE PAID BY ADDRESSEE

HARLEQUIN READER SERVICE
3010 WALDEN AVE
PO BOX 1867
BUFFALO NY 14240-9952

on this warm September evening. Cade found a key hidden beneath a ceramic rabbit that sat on the porch and he disappeared into the cabin. Joanna watched lights come on inside. Cade returned shortly.

"Lynne recently lost her husband. She's gone to Italy for a month. She won't mind our borrowing her little getaway shanty."

They carried their supplies into the house. Joanna realized it was decorated similarly to Cade's home— white oak floors and woodwork, wan leather furniture, everything understated, a seaside at winter, a water-color done in grays and whites. "Your friend apparently shares your decorating tastes."

Cade smiled. "Lynne helped me redecorate after the divorce."

"Oh." Joanna felt an unbidden twinge of jealousy. Had Cade consoled this unknown Lynne after her husband's death? The fact that she cared startled her. What Cade did with his friends—especially his women friends—was no business of hers.

Chiding herself, she strode across the hardwood floor and set the sacks she'd packed on the round oak table. The room was long, rectangular. The main level had a kitchen and living area combined. A staircase took up one end wall and a fireplace the other. Two doors opened on the back wall. The first was a bath-room/laundry room combination, the second was a large bedroom.

The only touch of whimsy was a white rocker in a corner that was surrounded by lush houseplants in assorted ceramic pots.

Along the hallway upstairs she saw four more doors. "Three small bedrooms and another bathroom," Cade said.

He set up Cody's new travel bed on the second floor in the middle room. Joanna noticed that the monochromatic color scheme was done throughout. Except for the plants, there was not so much as a single splash of warm hue to break up the monotony. She wondered what the woman who owned this house was like; there was little or nothing here to offer clues.

Cade said, "Take the end room, the one nearest the bathroom on this floor, and I'll take the one at the top of the stairs."

Her room consisted of a single wide chest of drawers in white oak, a matching double bed, a reading lamp attached to the headboard and a closet. She placed her new clothes on the dresser, then went to help Cade ready Cody for bed.

They were in the kitchen area. Cade was putting the baby-food jars on the counter. Joanna stopped halfway down the stairs. A smile warmed her. She'd give Cade a D− for mastering the right way of doing things, but an A+ for effort. He had Cody riding one hip as he reached into the sack with his free arm, the large man so dark and tanned, the tiny child so blond and fair. And yet, there was a natural balance in their contrasts, a secret harmony like notes of music for a song only her heart could sing.

He glanced up at her, and she felt suddenly self-conscious, aware of how badly she needed a shower, recalling his earlier dismissal of her disheveled appearance, remembering their kiss, however brief, as though it had seared her lips, branded her memory. She found her voice husky, uneven. "Need some help getting that little guy ready for bed?"

"I was trying to decide what to feed him."

"After all the French fries he's consumed, I think

he'd do well with a warm bath, some fresh sleepers and a bottle. The bath will help him sleep better in his new bed and these unfamiliar surroundings.''

''Yeah, he's had a lot of adjusting to do lately. The upstairs bathroom has a shower, but the one down here has a tub.''

''I was thinking of bathing him there.'' She glanced toward the huge single sink. ''It's definitely big enough.''

Cade raised his eyebrows, then nodded. ''Okay. I'll get a towel and washcloth. His shampoo and lotion are in the diaper bag.''

As Cade carried Cody to the downstairs bathroom, Joanna glanced around for the diaper bag, spotting it on the floor near the door. She caught the handles and was surprised at the weight. *What in the world?*

She reached into its depths and her fingertips hit something hard and steely. She brought it out. A gun clip full of bullets. Her mind flashed on the shot that had led to her father's death, she saw again that blink of light from the passing car, heard the awful bang, felt the glass exploding at her as the window blew inward. She shivered and tucked the clip back into the bottom of the diaper bag. No matter how safe she felt here, at this moment, they were not out of danger.

She heard Cade returning and retrieved the baby shampoo and lotion and carried them to the counter. Cade handed Cody to her, spread out the huge white bath towel and ran warm water in the sink. She laid the baby on the towel, then stripped off his clothing.

Cody kicked and squirmed and squeaked with delight. Typically male, he loved being naked, and she was struck anew by his beauty, his perfection. She grinned and touched his nose with affection, kissed his neck and cheek and lowered him into the sink. "You're such a handsome little guy."

Cody had no fear of the water. In fact, he seemed to love it. He slapped his hands against the surface, splashing her clothes and face. Laughing, Joanna drenched the washcloth in the water and tenderly drained it over her son's head and down his shoulders, thoroughly wetting him. Cody sucked in a sharp breath, then squealed and splashed her again. Her heart danced with joy. Their first time. Their first bath.

She lifted her gaze and met Cade's, his eyes were intense, that strange yearning had returned. She swallowed against the lump in her throat that his look caused. "Shampoo?"

He blinked, nodded, opened the flip cap, and she held out her palm. He squeezed a tiny pool of golden liquid into it. She rubbed it into Cody's hair, making certain that none ran into his eyes. The shampoo might be tearless, but she wasn't taking chances with this precious child.

Too soon, the pleasant task was done. She wrapped Cody into the big towel, gathered him to her and began gently buffing him. This part Cody found less fun than the bath. He fussed about getting dressed, but laughing and working together, Cade and she bested him.

Cody was cranky, tired, and grabbed on to his bottle as though they hadn't fed him in ages. As he suckled the warm liquid, his eyes sank to half-mast.

She carried him upstairs and laid him down in his new bed, then stood watching until he was asleep. Back in the hallway, she peered over the railing. The outside door was ajar. A bottle of wine stood open on the table with an empty glass beside it. Cade was not in the cabin.

She went down, poured herself some wine and found him on the porch, seated on the stairs that led down to a dock. The night was warm, the darkness softened by moonlight and stars, the quietude omnipotent, peaceful. She walked over to him. He raised his head. She said, "He's asleep."

Cade stared up at her, a glass of wine in his large hands. "You'll make a terrific mother. Your little girl is lucky."

"Lucky?" The word rushed from her, expelled by her guilt. All she could think was how unlucky this situation was.

Cade lifted his glass. "Don't look so sad. I promise you, we *will* find her."

Her stomach clenched. How could they look for her daughter when there was no daughter to look for? The ache to level with Cade swept through her, but she couldn't, wouldn't risk his acting differently, less fatherly to Cody. Everyone had to believe he was the boy's natural father, and in order for them to believe it, Cade had to believe it.

She swallowed a gulp of wine. "What are we going to do?"

"First, I'm going to talk to Addison."

"To what end?"

"I want to rattle his cage and see what falls out."

"You can't just walk in and accuse him and expect he'll let you get away with it."

"I know what I'm doing." His tone brooked no argument. "I need you to stay here with Cody. You'll be safe here. No one knows about this place. And I can't do what I have to do if I'm worried about my son...and you.''

She couldn't fully see his eyes, but she sensed the heat in them, that yearning she'd felt, identified with earlier. The wine was stealing her inhibitions, her resistance, making her long for the impossible, making her ache for the comfort of a man, this man.

JOANNA HAD PLANNED on dropping off to sleep the second her head hit the pillow. But sleep eluded her. She'd listened to Cade come inside, lock the cabin, set the alarm, then clump up to bed. He'd showered too. Then the cabin had gotten completely quiet. As the night grew long, she heard an owl hoot, then all was silent again.

In the silence, Cody cried out. Startled, she dashed out of bed, her bare feet hitting the cool hardwood floor. She was into the room and over to his crib in seconds. Moonlight stole through the window, bathing the baby in golden illumination. He was on his stomach, his little bottom in the air, his eyes closed.

She resisted the urge to touch him, to run her hand over his precious head. Sighing, she backed into the hallway and closed the door. Someone caught her from behind. She gasped, inhaling his scent, recognizing it. Cade. His solid chest and flat stomach pressed the length of her. His arms circled her, trapping her arms to her sides as he caught her in a bear hug. His nose bumped the top of her head. ''You.''

She squirmed in his hold, realizing belatedly how seductive the movements might be.

''Don't.'' His voice was a low growl, a raspy bark. With a start, she saw he was holding his gun. She froze. Carefully, he opened his arms, keeping the barrel pointed to the floor, sliding on the safety. "I'm sorry. I...I thought..." He nodded to Cody's room.

"He cried out. Must have had a nightmare. He's fast asleep." She hugged herself, then began to shake. "I...I don't like guns."

Cade set the Glock on the floor and moved to her. "I know. But until this mess is straightened out, it's necessary."

She swallowed and nodded, staring at her bare feet.

He thrust his finger under her chin and lifted it, raising her gaze to his. "You really should get some sleep. We both should."

She nodded again, but couldn't move, was trapped by the tiny connection of his finger touching her chin, trapped by the very male essence he exuded. She wanted to fall into his arms. Let him hold her and take this awful anxiety under control. Wanted to feel the heat of his naked chest penetrating her thin cotton T-shirt as though she wore nothing. Wanted to cling to him, to feel him grow hard with need. Wanted him to kiss her until she lost her senses, until her insides melted. She had never wanted a man this way.

Her thoughts galvanized her. She was so vulnerable. So needy. So desperate to feel something besides this constant fear and loneliness. But making love with a man she barely knew was something Joanna would never do again. Not in this lifetime.

No matter how desperately she wanted exactly that. And she did want that. Now. With Cade. She stepped back, pulling free of his hold on her, bid him goodnight and ran to her room.

CADE SPENT the rest of the night tossing and turning and intermittently dreaming of making love to Joanna.

He rose early, treated his unrelenting, unfulfilled desire to a long, cold shower. It was too early to try to get an appointment with Shane Addison. But he had to do something or he'd go mad.

He started the coffee, dialed the Issaquah Police Department and asked for Davis, his contact, hoping he was at work this early.

He got lucky. Davis answered right away. "I was hoping you'd call, Maconahey. I actually do have some news."

"All right." Cade pulled a mug from the cabinet. Finally a lead. A place to start. He had the feeling this was going to be a good day. "Lay it on me, buddy."

"We've identified some fingerprints in Nan's apartment."

"Great." He hoped they belonged to one of the thugs who'd visited his house yesterday. He really wanted to pin this on one of those guys. Would love the satisfaction of tying them together with Shane Addison *before* calling on the governor wannabe.

Cade poured coffee into his mug.

Davis cleared his throat, then said, "We got three partials and a full thumb." He told Cade where they'd found the prints. "They match the prints of the woman who owned the car they found Nancy's body in."

Cade dropped the full cup of coffee. It shattered in a dozen pieces—like his belief in the woman asleep upstairs. "Are you sure, Davis?"

"Positive. The prints belong to Joanna Edwards."

Chapter Nine

Joanna woke with a start to the sound of breaking glass. Her heart rate accelerated from zero to sixty in two seconds flat. She tossed back the covers, her first thought of Cody. Someone must have found them and broken in. She wrenched open her door and charged into the hallway.

The scent of coffee and movement in the room below pulled her up short. She pressed herself to the wall, inched down to her haunches and cautiously peered through the railing.

Cade was on his knees, mopping up spilled coffee, collecting the remnants of a shattered mug. She pushed out a breath of relief, then rose, her heartbeat slowing. She shoved her tousled hair off her face. "Have an accident?"

His head shot up. His gaze was dark, angry. At her? He said, "We need to talk."

"Well, sure." She frowned, disturbed at his gruffness. "Could I dress first?"

His gaze stole up her legs, and she suspected he had a very good view—that went higher than her T-shirt covered—from where he stood. His expression shifted, as though he was conflicted, torn between desire and a yearning to wring her neck. He said, "Yeah. That's a good idea. Make it quick."

She ignored the urgency in his voice. He might be in a bad mood, but she didn't have to join him. She stepped toward the baby's bedroom door. "Is Cody awake?"

"No." His tone was restrictive. Commanding. "Don't disturb him."

She stared down at him, hurt smarting her every nerve. Last night they'd agreed to trust one another. At the moment, she'd swear he had lost that trust. Why? What had happened? She returned to her room and donned a pair of khaki pants and a watercolor camp shirt and sandals.

In the austere bathroom, she brushed her hair off her face, applied mascara and lip gloss and studied her reflection. Her eyes flared with the fury that was building inside her. She strode downstairs. Cade stood at the window, looking out at the lake. Sunlight glistened off his thick sienna hair.

She poured herself a cup of coffee that rivaled the heat of her temper, then braced her hip against the counter. "What?"

Cade shifted toward her and she saw his hands were clenched, his eyes hot with emotions she couldn't name. He tilted his head, assessing her as though she were a novel whose plot he had figured out only to discover halfway through that he'd been wrong, fooled by a clever storyteller. "I called my friend at the Issaquah Police Department this morning."

"And?"

"He had some disturbing news for me."

She couldn't imagine anything more disturbing than the news that Nancy had been murdered, but apparently, there was more. Apparently something about *her*. "I thought you wanted to talk about it. Instead, you're making me pull it out of you. Why don't you just tell me?"

He tensed, his anger mounting at her challenge. Blow by blow, he related what Davis had told him. The whole time, his cerulean eyes studied her, darkening as he spoke, turning stormy. But somehow, he seemed as irked with himself as he was with her.

She blew out a furious breath. "I don't care what your friend Davis discovered, it cannot be. I've never been to Nancy's apartment. I don't even know where it is."

"Don't you?" He eyed her pointedly. "You were trying to find her. You found me."

"Yes, I did." She stiffened. "My cousin Kenner found you on the Internet. He had no luck finding Nancy. That's why I came to you. Hoping you'd know where to locate her."

He stepped toward her. "Then how did your fingerprints end up inside her apartment?"

"How should I know?" She wanted to scream. "Even you have to see this frame is cheap enough to suit a velvet painting."

"Funny you should mention a painting."

"Not so funny when you consider it's what I do. I'm a painter—as in artist, remember."

"Ironic, I meant."

"Explain."

"Your fingerprints were found on a painting." He strode past her, pulled a fresh mug from the cupboard and filled it with coffee. "A painting Nan had on her living-room wall."

Joanna opened her mouth and clamped it shut.

Dumbfounded. How could her fingerprints be in Nancy's apartment, on a painting? She stared at Cade, who seemed to be waiting for her to admit she'd lied to him. But she knew she hadn't. So what explained this? A wayward thought occurred to her, and her pulse skipped. *Was it possible?* "What of?"

"What of?" He shook his head, not understanding.

Her grip tightened on her mug and she spoke slowly. "What is the painting of?"

He plowed a hand through his hair. Squinted. His expression was contemplative, as though he was envisioning something in his mind's eye. "It was kind of fuzzy, as though the colors were blurred and smudged."

"An acrylic?"

He shrugged. "You got me. It was all blues and yellows and pinks. Suited Nan's tastes to a tee."

"What was the picture of?"

"I don't know. A city, maybe."

"Downtown Spokane?"

"Yeah, maybe."

"And did you see the signature?"

"Signature?"

"The artist's signature."

He thought again, then nodded, seeming surprised that he recalled. "I think it was Joe."

"J.O.E. Initials. *My initials.*"

"Your—" He broke off. His eyes widened as what she was telling him sank in. "You're Joe?"

"Joanna Orville Edwards. I sign all of my paintings J.O.E."

The light of anger in his eyes wavered. "What was Nan doing with one of your paintings? Did she buy it? Did you give it to her?"

Did she steal it? Joanna nearly snapped at him. Trying to haul in her temper, she said, "I did not give it to her. I've got as much idea of how it ended up in her apartment as I do of how my fingerprints were on it after all this time." Anger still singed her words. She didn't like being attacked the way he'd attacked her.

"Fingerprints can stay on an item for years," Cade said, his own voice losing its hard edge. "There's no telling when they got there. Yours were found on the frame that the canvas was stretched to."

"I stretch my own canvases."

Silence fell between them, the air electric with the force of their personal efforts to rein in their tempers, to reassess their tenuous relationship.

Joanna sipped her coffee. The jolt of caffeine and heat hit her system together, bolstering her. "She must have taken it from my studio. It's an old one and I hadn't noticed it was missing."

She hadn't noticed anything after the loss of her baby. She'd spent months in despair, months in self-pity, barely aware of anything. She'd gone into the studio seldom. When she did, she would lose herself in her painting, but everything she'd created these last five months was dark and gloomy. Her best work, Luna said. The art had an edge, a maturity that had been missing before.

Cade drank his coffee down. "According to Ted, Nan hasn't been at her apartment in about eleven months. When did she hang that painting?"

"It must have been before my baby was born then."

"How did she come by it? I can't believe she'd steal it."

He didn't want to believe Nan had stolen her baby

either, she realized. Because if he did, he might have to wonder why she'd take one baby when she had one of her own.

"Maybe my father gave it to her for a bonus. He was always telling anyone who'd listen that they'd be wise to buy my paintings now while they were affordable as I was going to be 'famous' one day."

Her voice cracked as she realized for all of his controlling ways, her father had also been her biggest supporter. "He wasn't much of a salesman. Didn't sell a single painting. But he really did believe in me."

Cade looked as though he envied her having a parent who believed in her. He refilled his cup. "Well, I'm no art critic. Roses are my thing. But Nan probably liked the painting because it's all pastels."

Recalling the acrylic, she thought he was probably right.

He continued, "Meanwhile the price on your head has doubled and the search for your whereabouts increased to a frenzy."

"You didn't tell Davis I was here with you?"

"No."

If the tables had been reversed, she wasn't sure whether or not she would have handed him over with the amount of glaring evidence piling up. She knew then that he hadn't lost his core belief in her innocence. If he had, if he did, he wouldn't hesitate to turn her over to his peers.

She glanced outside, at the sun-kissed lake, and thought how free she seemed at this moment. When all the while an unseen net was sneaking closer and closer around her. She couldn't just sit here and do nothing. Couldn't allow Cade to step into the fray without her. She owed him.

Again their gazes met and locked, and she felt the huge gulf of minutes ago lessening. But an unspoken cease-fire wasn't enough for her. "Cade, I won't have you trusting me with your son one moment, then telling me to stay away from him the next. Shane Addison is trying to frame me for this murder and either you believe I'm one hundred percent innocent all the time or not at all. You need to make up your mind now or I'm out that door. Which is it?"

He tipped his head, surprised at her ultimatum, but respect filled his eyes. "Stay. I know you didn't kill Nan. But I don't think you can blame my motives. How would you have reacted if you'd gotten this news about me? I just met you. I have a little boy who's just lost his mother to think about. First and foremost, I have his best interests to consider. Not yours. And not mine."

"I know." She had no right to expect more from him than he was already giving her. But at the moment she needed his trust, his full trust, or she would lose Cody again. Would lose him permanently. "Okay, I'll stay."

"And I won't jump to any more conclusions—no matter where the facts point."

The last of her anger dissipated. "Promise?"

He nodded, sincerity in his look, his stance, the set of his strong jaw. "Yes."

The moment was punctuated by Cody, who hollered, "Dadadadadadadadadadadadada."

Cade's mouth lifted at the corners and the smile went all the way to his eyes. "See, my son is telling you to believe me."

Joanna grinned. "Why do they always learn 'dada' first?"

Cade ignored her question. "I've got to make a phone call, would you mind getting Cody?"

Mind? Never. She set her cup on the counter and said in a teasing voice, "You just don't want to deal with his morning diaper."

"I'm no dummy," Cade teased in return. "It might take me a couple of times, but eventually I figure things out."

As she climbed the stairs, she knew he was not talking about just the diaper, but her. Knew he would no longer doubt her, mistrust her. And yet, he should distrust her—because she was telling him the biggest lie of all. Joanna's guilt lay heavy on her heart.

"I COULDN'T GET an appointment to see our favorite candidate, but I learned he's speaking today at a luncheon for the League of Women Voters at the Lady Diana Hotel in downtown Seattle. So, if I can't see him at his office, I'll go to where he's lunching." Cade hung up the phone and jammed his hand through his hair. "The trick will be getting close enough to talk to him."

Joanna glanced up from feeding Cody rice cereal. She met Cade's eyes. "I'll get you close enough."

"What?" His eyebrows lifted and he began shaking his head. "Oh, no. You're not budging an inch from this place."

"He won't let you near." She spooned more cereal into Cody's mouth, kissing his head. "His bodyguards won't let you near. And you don't want to shout what you have to say to him, do you?"

"No." Cade's face was suffused with color. "But I don't want Cody in the line of fire."

Joanna gave him a sharp narrow-eyed look. "Do

you think I do? You're not a stupid man, Cade. Don't start acting like it. Shane Addison is the top gubernatorial candidate at a luncheon of women voters. He won't pull anything on us. It would be political suicide. In fact, out of fear that I'll blab to the press, he'll agree to speak to me in private, if only for a few minutes.''

''And you're not a stupid woman. What if someone recognizes you before we get his attention? What if his 'bodyguards' call the police and tell them where to find you?''

She blew out her breath and caught Cody's hand just as his fingertips landed in the mush. She wiped them off on his bib. She considered Cade's objection. ''I'll go in disguise. All you'll have to do is get his attention. Then I'll reveal myself and we can talk to him alone.''

''Once that happens, the cops and everyone else will know my involvement with you. I can kiss my career and my pension goodbye.''

''Of course, I hadn't thought about that.'' Damn. There had to be some way around that problem. He might not realize it, yet, but he did need her help. She nodded. ''Okay. Then you use my name to get his attention. While you're talking to him, I'll play lookout.''

''Lookout?'' He seemed amused.

''Yes, lookout. I'll keep an eye out for those guys who came to your house yesterday. I'll be able to warn you, call your cell phone or something, if one of the bodyguards decides to make mincemeat out of you.''

Cade smirked. ''You watch too much television.''

''It'll work. You need backup.

He scowled at her. ''I don't do partners.''

"I thought all cops had partners."

"You *do* watch too much television."

She wouldn't justify that with a response. She made a face at him, then presented Cody with another spoonful of cereal. The baby refused the offering. She pushed the bowl aside and rose, carted her son to the sink and wiped his mouth with a clean cloth. "You didn't see the men who came to your house yesterday. Only *I* can point them out to you."

Cade pressed his lips together, tight. "Damn it, I don't like this." But his argument held little bite. He poured a fresh cup of coffee and stalked out to the dock.

Joanna finished feeding Cody and soon had him in the sink for his morning bath. As she scrubbed him, she realized she was beginning to know the planes and angles of his tiny body. Every sweep of her hand over him gave her a burst of elation, small explosions of bliss.

But every time she glanced up at Cade, guilt flattened her pleasure. He was a good man. A good father. A good friend. At the moment, he seemed like a man with the weight of the world on his shoulders. She supposed he was. Thanks to her.

"Mamamamamamamama," Cody prattled, jerking her attention back to him.

"Well, young man, your 'mama' is right here and she's doing her darnedest to make a future for the two of us."

He slapped his hand on the water, splattering her shirtfront. Laughing and chiding him without meaning it, she lifted him to the fresh towel and went through the squirm-and-grab ritual of dressing him, this time in a blue T-shirt and short coveralls. She left his feet bare.

Cade came back inside and she could see he'd made up his mind. "Okay, but I'll carry Cody in the new backpack. You'll have to go into the building, disguised and as though you aren't with us. At the first sign that someone is paying you undue attention, do whatever you need to protect yourself. You'll have my cell phone number and we'll hook up later if we get separated."

"Okay." Joanna felt a rush of excitement. Finally she was going to be taking action instead of standing by waiting for Shane Addison to act against her. This was the first step toward regaining her life.

"What kind of disguise are you going to wear?" Cade asked.

"Since it's a woman's luncheon at the Lady Diana Hotel, I can hardly go like this, or in my only other outfit, jeans and a baseball cap."

"With sunglasses to hide your lovely face." He traced the contour of her cheek as he said this and her skin heated in response to his moving fingertip, kindling a fire deep within her belly.

Flustered, and fearing she might act on the urge to step into his arms, on the sudden intense yearning to taste his kiss again, she handed Cody to him. "If we have to shop, we'd better get a move on."

"This way, then." Instead of heading toward the door, he strode into the bedroom on the main floor. He glanced back at her. "Come on."

She followed.

He crossed to the walk-in closet and opened the double doors, revealing a wealth of clothes and shoes and hats. "I thought maybe we'd see what Lynne has that we could borrow. She's a couturiere, designs clothes and sells them on the Internet from her Web page. She wears her own designs, and as you can see, she's fond of dresses and hats. You think something like that would do? I mean, you're about the same size as she.''

Joanna blanched and a flush of heat burned in her tummy. She ought to be flattered being compared to a woman Cade obviously respected and admired. But she wasn't and that shook her to her toes. She was starting to care more about Cade Maconahey than was good for either of them. That simply would not do.

She groaned silently. It was wrong. She was going to break his heart. He was going to hate her—almost as much as she hated herself—for allowing him to believe that Cody was his son. She said, ''Let's see what there is.''

She moved past Cade, catching his delicious scent, ignoring it with an effort, pushing her gaze and her attention toward the clothes in the closet. If Lynne's couturiere taste was anything like her taste in decorating, Joanna was sure she'd hate whatever this closet held.

To her surprise, she found she liked Lynne's clothes, which tended to Calvin Klein simplicity of color and style. The hats showed a frivolous streak, not in their pale hues, but in the designs.

She chose an ecru sheath and a straw hat with a brim so wide it drooped down around her face on both sides, effectively hiding her profile. Lynne's shoes were too large. Her own sandals would have to do.

In the bathroom, she applied makeup, and with her artist's expertise refocused the attention of her face, made her eyes appear slanted, her cheekbones higher.

She outlined her lips, making them seem larger, then filled in the area with bloodred lipstick.

She found some nail polish that matched the red lipstick and painted her finger- and toenails. The sheath she borrowed fit like a glove. If she hadn't lost weight, she'd never have squeezed into this woman's clothes. It made her wonder if Lynne was one of those "you can never be too rich or too thin" advocates.

She pulled her hair completely off her face, pinning the longer strands off her neck so that none of it peeked beneath the hat. Satisfied with the finished look, she walked into the kitchen, where Cade was putting Cody in his car seat. Cade's eyes shone with approval. He whistled. "You look like a completely different woman."

"That was the whole idea." Her cheeks heated at his complimentary tone. He made her feel good about herself as she hadn't for far too long. Made her feel confident. Clever. Pretty. Needed.

He lifted the car seat. Cody was enjoying his bottle and falling asleep. Once in the SUV, he would conk out hard. She smiled. Cade said, "Let's go."

ON THE DRIVE to Seattle, Cade changed their plans. Joanna would take Cody. He'd have to use his position as a Seattle police detective to penetrate the inner circle of security that would be protecting Shane Addison. Toting a baby in a backpack would lend him little credence.

He gave her his cell phone number, advised her to make note of pay phone areas in the hotel and offered her a fistful of coins. He closed his hand reassuringly over hers and the contact stirred those feelings she wanted to squelch, wanted to deny, wanted to act on.

Every minute they spent together made it harder, made the need deeper, brought the memory of his lips on hers, brought the desire to be with him, to kiss him again and again...and again.

It was one-thirty by the time they reached downtown.

"Looks like the whole Northwest decided to spend this glorious day walking and driving in Seattle," Cade observed.

Sidewalks and streets alike were packed. Cade tried three parking lots before finding a space in one that also rented wheelchairs and strollers. It was four blocks from the Lady Diana.

Joanna rented a stroller for Cody. The afternoon was warm, filled with the scents of exhaust and salty sea air. She followed half a block behind Cade, entering the hotel a minute after him.

The lobby, a two-story tribute to elegant hotels of the forties, was strangely subdued considering the event occurring in the tenth-floor ballroom. Joanna watched Cade head toward the escalators. She would take the elevator. She propelled the stroller across the floor, a mosaic designed in charcoal and white marble intersected by velvetlike slabs of carpet in an old rose and red wine diamond pattern. Walls and counters were paneled in dark cherry wood.

She kept her eyes peeled looking for the sweating man and the man with the scar. Cade thought the men might be acting as security. Security, he'd warned her, would be easy to spot. Their job was more about discouraging interlopers than actually confronting or engaging in any conflict with them. She saw neither man on the main floor.

Joanna pressed the up button for the elevator. Cody

was awake. His little head pivoted back and forth, his gaze taking in everything, all of it new and interesting to him. She maneuvered the stroller to the back of the empty elevator and selected the tenth floor.

The doors slid shut and the elevator began to rise. Cody frowned, his mouth puckered and his little body tensed. The motion was new and not to his liking.

"It's okay, sweetie." She squatted so he could see her face as she spoke reassuringly to him. Like a kitten fascinated by a jiggling string, Cody focused on her bobbing hat. In a blink, he grabbed the brim in his tight grip. She felt the hat slip.

"No, no, Cody, let go." Gingerly, she freed the hat from his grasp. The elevator stopped on the third floor. The doors swung open. Joanna blanched, half stood, caught her reflection in the mirrored walls. Her hair showed in the front.

A couple boarded and immediately remarked on what a handsome little boy they thought Cody was. Joanna thanked them, swiftly and deftly readjusted the hat, then glanced at the couple. Her heart skipped two beats. She knew this woman, and this man from TV and newspapers.

She was Shane Addison's wife, Kendall. *He* was Mel Reagan, Addison's personal assistant. Either could have orchestrated the attacks on her father and her.

A clammy chill swept Joanna's body. *Stay calm,* she told herself. But how could she?

Kendall Addison was gazing at her as though she recognized her, but couldn't place her face with her name. Yet.

Chapter Ten

Joanna's gaze was locked with Kendall Addison's. Kendall, she noted, liked yellow. Yellow hair, yellow suit, yellow shoes. She looked like a sunflower stretching toward the unseen sky. Her eyes were like the seeds of the flower, burned brown. She appeared poised, held together by stress and ambition.

Joanna wanted to look away, but the fear in her belly had spread to her limbs, frozen her in place. The elevator began to ascend. Cody made another distressed cry. It snapped Joanna's lethargy. *Cody!* What if Kendall Addison noticed his resemblance to Shane?

She hunched down, blocking him, hiding him, offering him words of comfort in a gentle voice. As he calmed, she risked a glance over her shoulder.

Kendall was no longer watching her. No longer wondering why she seemed familiar? Joanna swallowed past the lump in her throat. Kendall stood close enough to Mel Reagan to touch him, but didn't touch him, as though she were not touching him on purpose, not in public anyway. She spoke just above a whisper, nodding toward the open newspaper in Reagan's hand. "Have you taken care of that little problem?"

From where she crouched, Joanna could not see the

paper, but she knew her photo was likely on the front page. She shifted her attention to the man.

Mel Reagan was not handsome in any classic way. His face was pitted, his eyes too black, his hair receding at both temples. But there was something about him, an energy that begged to be noticed, pondered, partaken of. The perfect politician.

Yet, he stayed in the shadows. Never aspiring to office? Perhaps his background would not withstand the scrutiny of a voracious press attack if ever he threw his hat in the ring.

Mel studied Kendall's perfectly made-up face. "Actually, not yet. But I'm working on it. Everyone denies involvement. Denies knowing who put out the directives." His voice was as smooth as hard candy. "But I will find and eliminate your concerns. I promise."

"Good. I want her dealt with, swiftly and finally, once and for all. I won't have this—" She broke off and glanced toward Joanna as though she'd only just recalled they weren't alone in the elevator. She smiled, the proper first lady of the state, then glanced at Mel. "I won't have Susan throwing tantrums and disrupting the preparations for the charity art auction this Friday. Imagine a nine-year-old wanting to go to private school. The public school systems might not be perfect, but they're good enough for our voters, and good enough for our daughters."

Joanna caught the phony smile Kendall gave Mel in the mirror. The candidate's wife figured she'd covered herself with a plausible lie. Anyone other than Joanna might have fallen for the diversion. But Joanna realized the "her" Kendall Addison wanted dealt with swiftly and finally was Joanna herself.

Her heart raced and fury burned through her, fury

and an icy fear, the coldhearted menace made more chilling by the fact that this woman could speak of having someone murdered and her own child in the same breath.

The elevator stopped with a tiny jolt. The doors swept open. They were on the ninth floor. Mel and Kendall stepped off. Kendall told him, ''I'm quite excited about the auction we're hosting at the mansion. The new artist I've discovered does the most incredible things with jewelry and accessories. I've been touting his work to everyone. Giving it as gifts. He's so clever.''

Knowing the conversation would soon revert to her demise, Joanna wanted to follow them, to eavesdrop further, to learn what they planned for her next in order to circumvent it.

But she couldn't risk Kendall taking a better look at her, perhaps realizing who she was looking at.

With an effort, Joanna stayed put, watching them stride down the hall, their heads bent together. Neither glanced back at her, dismissing the woman in the floppy brimmed hat as though she and her son had nothing to do with either of them.

As the elevator doors glided shut, Joanna laughed with relief, sank to her haunches and kissed her son's cheek. ''That was too close for comfort, sweetie.''

Cody's eyebrows dipped as the elevator began rising once again, his mouth forming a pucker. She reassured him, held his hand, touched his cheek. He grabbed for her finger, distracted, his fear forgotten. The door opened on the tenth floor and she rose, gathering her composure with effort.

This was not a hallway of hotel rooms, but a vast open walkway and gathering area that led to the grand ballroom. She spied three doors into the ballroom, each guarded by two husky-looking men. None was either of the two who had scared her yesterday morning at Cade's house.

Cade was nowhere in sight. Her ride in the elevator had taken longer than anticipated. Some lookout she was. Had Cade already penetrated the front line of security and made it into the inner circle? Was he talking to Shane at this very minute?

She moved out of the elevator, feeling, more than seeing, the heads of all six guards snap toward her. Her pulse tripped. She murmured, "What do we do now, Cody?"

She pushed the stroller forward, passed the first two sets of doors. A burst of applause from inside the ballroom was followed by an explosion of voices colliding in conversation. The guards shoved the ballroom doors open. Women began to stream out, a vast flow of moving bodies in all shapes and sizes, a sea of suits and dresses and slacks.

Fearing they'd be trampled, Joanna steered the stroller out of the path of disaster and to the far end wall away from the elevators. Arriving there, she spotted another hallway, this one running parallel to the ballroom. Another door was inset halfway down. Two more guards stood there.

They were talking to each other. Joanna's hands locked on the stroller as recognition flowed hot through her, burning her to the spot where she stood. The crush of racket from the departing audience drowned out any noise that might have alerted them to Joanna's and Cody's approach.

The taller of the two men was mopping his forehead with a huge hankie, sweating even in the air-conditioned hotel. The other man's face was hidden from her, but she knew if he turned so she could see his face there would be a scar through his left eyebrow.

Her pulse slammed against her temples. Here was the proof Cade kept harping on. Proof that the men who'd stolen her car worked for Shane Addison.

The men glanced at her, breaking the thread of apprehension that held her in place. She dipped her head, wheeled the stroller in the opposite direction and, trying to make herself move without running, marched toward the elevators. She heard footsteps behind her. The guards. One or both? She risked a glance around. Both. They were moving slowly, stealthily, focused on her.

Fear brushed the small of her back. She picked up her step, hurrying to the elevators. She had to find Cade. Had to tell him. As she came abreast of the first ballroom door, Shane Addison stepped from within, right into her path. Joanna halted as though someone had jerked her from behind. She was trapped, snagged like a bug on a lizard's tongue.

She forgot about the men behind her. Her attention was riveted on the man who had once told her he loved her then turned her life upside down into a living hell. Her mouth dried and the hatred seared through her.

He caught sight of her, a ready smile as false as his promises lifted the corners of his mouth. A flash of lust entered his hazel eyes, but not recognition. At that moment, she was nothing more to him than another possible conquest.

Her rage grew to a bonfire, searing red behind her eyes, slashing through her. She stepped toward him, as though she were accepting his unspoken, indecent proposal, unable to stop herself. She would slap that leer off his face.

Behind her, she heard the men nearing.

Behind Shane, someone said, "Thank you, Mr. Addison."

Cade. Joanna lowered her gaze, but not before watching Shane pull his own gaze reluctantly from her. She fastened her hands tighter on the stroller handle. Forced her feet to move.

Shane said, "Sorry you've wasted your time, Officer Maconahey. But it's comforting to know Seattle's finest are doing everything possible to find this woman. The fact that she imagines she had an intimate relationship with me shows how deranged she is. I've never even met the woman."

Joanna's head came up at that. Fury flashed from her eyes. She stumbled a step forward. Cade moved quicker. "Ah, there you are, darling."

Before she could react, he swept her into his arms as though it were the most natural thing in the world, pulling her shocked body against his hard muscles, one of his hands cupped her head, holding the hat in place. His mouth found hers and took possession.

The fire from his lips burned hotter than her rage, melted every thought of revenge on Shane Addison from her mind, his image, his name, dissolved every fear of the two guards who'd stolen her car and likely murdered Nancy. All she saw behind her closed eyes was Cade Maconahey, all she felt was his lips on hers, his arms around her, his big, warm, reassuring arms, his kiss forcing life into her veins, flames into her blood, blazing zings of heat through every part of her.

The tension left her, and she seemed to soften

against him, molding to every plane and angle of his body, the fit perfect, preordained, as though designed by nature long before they'd ever met. She wanted the wonder of it to go on forever.

Too soon, he lifted his head, breaking the contact. Her breath tangled with his, escaping in pure sweet-flavored sighs. She felt stunned, smacked with desire from her head to her feet, the sensation new, something she'd never before experienced. Not in Paris, not with Shane, never with Bob.

Who was this man, Cade Maconahey, that he could reach inside her soul, touch her in such intimate ways when he didn't know her at all, hadn't touched her intimately at all?

His hold on her remained taut. She was grateful, certain she could never have stood on her own at this moment. There was a warning in his gaze, and a reprimand. His voice was hoarse, gruff, low. He murmured, "Whew. You damn near blew the whole thing. What were you thinking? Just what did you hope to accomplish by confronting Addison?"

"Confronting? Hell, I wanted to smack that filthy leer off his face." She shook herself. "He didn't even recognize me."

"Is that what you wanted him to do?"

"No, I...I...I just saw red." She shuddered, unable to bear thinking what might have happened if Cade hadn't stopped her with his kiss. She touched her lips; they felt swollen, bruised. She grappled with the rampant yearnings still running wild through her. "Thank you for...stopping me."

His eyes narrowed and his expression heated, his gaze moving over her like the feathering touch of a lover. "I don't consider that kiss a stop but a start...of something that we cannot explore or continue here."

His grin held a promise that he would explore, would continue this later. She was shocked at the anticipation that promise stirred. As she struggled to find her poise, he stepped back and mussed his hair with those big wonderful hands.

They were alone in the wide hallway, she realized. The massive crowd had cleared out like sand from the top of an hourglass. Even the guards were gone.

Cade said, "Well, this was a waste of time. Addison denied everything."

"I heard. But it wasn't a waste, Cade. I saw the two men who were at your house yesterday. The ones who stole my car and likely killed Nancy. They work for Shane. They were guarding one of the entrances to the ballroom. They were following me. Did you notice them?"

"Did one of them have a sweat-gland problem?"

"Yes."

"That was one of the reasons I grabbed you. They looked ready to pounce on you. Why were they following you?"

"I'm not sure. I didn't think either of them had seen my face. Maybe they just wanted to check me out. Find out what I was doing near that back entrance."

"Probably." Cade agreed. "If they were sure who you were, they'd have told Addison and it would all be over but the shouting."

Her stomach dipped and she told Cade about running into Kendall and Mel Reagan in the elevator. He said, "Let's get out of here before we have any more close encounters."

She nodded and glanced down at her son. Cody was

looking from one to the other of them, his eyes saucer-size. As he caught her attention, he grinned that great wide innocent smile that made the earth tilt and settle, that made sense of the absurd, that made every struggle on his behalf worth the effort.

Cade caught the handle of the stroller and began moving toward the elevators. "We've got to prove those men work for Addison. Find a paper trail, phone records or something."

On the descent to the lobby, she said, "We need to buy a newspaper. I have an idea that just might get us inside the Addison mansion."

ON THE WAY to the parking garage, they purchased the *Seattle Times*. Joanna waited until they were in Lynne's SUV, merging with traffic on Fourth Avenue before she spread the paper on her lap. Her photo stared up at her. Nancy's murder and the hunt for Joanna were the lead stories. She was a fugitive, considered dangerous, maybe armed. The whole thing was ridiculous. Mind-boggling. Terrifying.

She forced her gaze away from that story and found the one about the charity art auction. As she'd hoped, the galleries that would be contributing were listed. She scanned the list, then smiled. Galleria de Cassili was there.

"So, what's this idea of yours?" Cade asked.

"The Addisons are hosting an art auction for charity. One of the contributors is my friend, Luna Cassili, the gallery owner. The one I told you about."

"The one who's trying to sell your watercolors?"

"Yes. She might be able to get us invited."

"To an art auction? Why would we want to do that?"

"Because it's being held at the Addison mansion. If we can gain admission into their residence, we can slip away from the party and into the private section of the house. It will give us the opportunity to look for phone records and other evidence of Shane's or Kendall's involvement in the attacks against me and my father."

"Why would we be given invitations?"

"Artists are invited as well as art patrons. Luna will have invitations to disperse."

"Does it not occur to you that the police will be all over a function like that expecting you to show up?"

"Why? The police who are looking for me don't know about my accusations against Shane. And if most cops are even half as smart as you, they aren't likely to think I'm dumb enough to show up at an art event when my face is so recognizable."

"Compliments won't sway me." But his frown told her she was swaying him. "You'll be in disguise, of course."

"Yes, and what makes my plan so brilliant is that I'll be hiding in plain sight."

They were at a stoplight. She turned and looked at Cody in the back. He was sucking on his bottle, the motion of the car making him drowsy.

"How good a friend is this Luna Cassili?" Cade's expression was somber, concerned. "Will she turn you over to the police if you contact her?"

"No."

"Are you sure?"

The underlying query beneath his question jolted her. He was asking if she knew who her real friends were. A sickening sensation swept her as she realized there would be those among her small circle of intimates who would believe the news reports, who would be shocked, but who would not doubt the evidence as presented.

At the moment, she could almost name those who would and wouldn't condemn her without hearing her side. But Luna? No. Luna would keep an open mind and wait for Joanna to tell her what had happened. "Luna and I met in junior high school. The summer before, when she was only thirteen, she'd had a baby and given it up for adoption. The stress of the ordeal cost Luna all of her hair. Alopecia. The other kids treated her as if she had some contagious disease. They were cruel beyond belief. Except for me. I admired her spirit and her outlook and we became fast friends."

Joanna folded the newspaper and set it on the seat between herself and Cade. "Her hair has never come back, a constant reminder of that time. She wears wigs and false eyelashes now. She has never forgotten my loyalty. She won't judge me, won't believe me guilty unless I tell her I'm guilty."

"Then call her." He handed her his cell phone.

She thought a moment, then dialed. Luna answered on the third ring. Without speaking, Joanna hung up. "She's there. But I won't risk talking to her on the phone. This must be done in person. Her gallery is on Second Avenue." She gave Cade directions.

They pulled to the curb across the street from Galleria de Cassili. Cade studied the shop, stuck between a bookstore and a deli. "Would she have tried to contact you when this news broke?"

"Undoubtedly."

"The police would know about her then."

Joanna's pulse shimmied. "You think they're watching her shop?"

"Neither Tukwila nor Seattle has the manpower to cover everyone they suspect you might contact. But you can bet she's been interviewed and advised to call if she hears from you."

"Okay." Joanna checked her appearance in the visor mirror and freshened her lipstick. "I'll go in alone. You stay here with Cody."

"No. We'll go together. As far as we know, no one is looking for a family of three."

They waited until it appeared Joanna's friend was alone in the shop. Cade strapped on the baby carrier and Joanna adjusted the baby into it. Cody kept trying to grab her hat. Grinning at him, she stepped out of his reach.

Here, as near the hotel, sidewalks and streets were crowded with people enjoying the warm afternoon. As Cade and Joanna crossed the street, she said, "Don't be surprised at Luna's appearance. I never know whether to expect a blonde, redhead or brunette. Depends on her mood and the wig of the day."

A bell announced their entrance into the shop. The gallery was shallow, but broad with myriad art pieces displayed on walls, screens and stands, everything from metal sculptures to framed collages, blown glassware to carved whalebone, jewelry to paintings.

They wove their way through the creative eclectic maze to a counter against the side wall. Luna Cassili stood beside a cash register, jotting in a ledger of some kind.

Even forewarned, Cade was surprised by her appearance. If her hair was a wig it was the best he'd ever seen, long, flowing to her shoulders in a shade of crimson he'd only seen on autumn leaves. She was small-boned, tiny, a fairy queen with delicate features and a wreath of summer flowers circling her head like a sweatband. A dress that looked straight out of the hippie generation hugged her slender frame.

For such a tiny woman, she exuded a presence that was larger than life. She was the most eye-catching piece of art in her shop, and he felt this was deliberate on her part.

She glanced up as they approached, her discerning gaze taking in the total picture; a family with means, it said.

"Luna." Joanna's voice trembled. Cade held his breath, praying her belief in this woman wasn't misplaced.

Luna's expression altered. "Joanna? Is that you? Oh my God, it is."

She rushed from behind the counter and swept her arms around Joanna. Cade released a taut breath, impressed at this show of absolute unquestioning belief in Joanna's innocence.

The door to the shop opened. Joanna and Luna reacted as though someone had dropped one of those expensive glass bowls near the front of the gallery.

Cade wheeled in the direction of the door. An expensively dressed African-American woman was studying a metal sculpture. A customer from the look of her. His pulse slowed to normal. Cody jabbered, reaching for a shelf of carved bone that Cade had stepped too near.

"My office," Luna whispered. "I'll be right in."

Joanna caught Cade's hand, avoiding any glance toward the newcomer.

"Customer," he whispered.

She nodded and led him into Luna's office at the back of the shop. They left the door ajar in order to hear what was going on. This area, nearly as large as the shop space, doubled as a storage room. Unlike the asymmetrical arrangement of the gallery, here there was order, obsessive neatness. Crates and boxes were aligned, labeled and stacked in rows, with room to navigate between them.

An antique rolltop desk hugged one wall. On its surface was a laptop computer, a portable phone, a pile of orders and a pen. Luna was a stickler for detail and couldn't work amid clutter.

Joanna stood near Cade, playing with Cody. In the other room, they heard Luna offer to assist the customer who said she was ''just looking.'' She ''looked'' for ten minutes. They heard the bell over the door tinkle and a moment later Luna joined them.

She said, ''I've put up the Closed sign, but if it's on too long, someone is liable to get suspicious. There's been a cop in here checking with me yesterday and today. I wouldn't be surprised if he returns.'' She eyed Cade and the baby, her skillfully penciled eyebrows flinching. ''Joanna, is this your daughter?''

''No,'' Cade answered. ''He's my son, Cody. I'm Cade Maconahey.''

Luna started. ''The cop?'' Her gaze flew from him to Joanna. ''Nancy Wheeler's ex?''

''Yes,'' Joanna confirmed.

''Yow.'' She glanced from one to the other of them again. ''Which of you is going to explain why, with every cop in King County looking for you, this one hasn't turned you in?''

Joanna blew out a breath. ''Luna, the story is too long and we've too little time at the moment.''

"Okay. Sure, okay. So, how can I help?"

Joanna explained about the invitations to the charity art auction, and why they needed to get into the Addisons' mansion. "I'd like you to contribute my two watercolors to the affair."

"No can do." Luna shook her head. "Oh, the invitations are no problem. I have those here." She reached into her desk and withdrew two gilt-edged envelopes. "But this morning I sold both of your paintings. Snatched up by a collector who expects their value to soar if you're caught and convicted."

Joanna winced. "Seems my dad was wrong. I'm not going to be famous, but infamous."

Luna patted her hand. "Look at it this way, you've sold your first two paintings. It's a beginning. And if it makes you feel better, I gouged the jerk for his stupidity. Turned a nice profit for me and a nicer one for you."

"I guess that's something." Joanna had expected this moment to be elating. Instead, she couldn't even enjoy it.

"As far as the auction goes, I have to account for every artist invitation I give out. So, I need merchandise to coincide with the invitations. I can't risk substituting someone else's work, as everyone I represent in the gallery is already attending the auction. But if you can get me another painting or two by Friday, I'll add them to those I'm contributing."

"Wait a minute, ladies." Cade scowled. "If you submit paintings with Joanna listed as the artist, they'll likely be rejected."

Luna pursed her tiny lips. "I daresay he's right. But, you know, Joanna, since you sign your work only with your initials, I could submit them under a false name.

That will account for my giving out two invitations to my new discovery, er, ah, J. Owen Eagle.''

"J. Owen Eagle?" Joanna shook her head. "I guess that's all right." She glanced at Cade and Luna. "But all of my other paintings are in my studio in Spokane."

"Then we'll get them." Cade shifted his shoulders, the baby pack getting uncomfortable. "We can't afford to pass up this opportunity."

"Good." Luna opened her checkbook. "I'll pay you now for the two you've sold. I'm sure, under the circumstances, you could use the money."

"No." Cade warned. "That would be proof that you'd seen her. You could go to jail for harboring a criminal."

Luna narrowed her gaze at him. "Is that the pot calling the kettle black?"

"You have no idea," Joanna said. "He's risking more for me than I can ever repay."

Luna looked intrigued, but didn't ask for details; Joanna knew she expected those would be shared with her when the timing was better.

"Well, the auction is black-tie. Will you have trouble getting formal wear?"

"We'll rent if we have to." Cade offered.

Luna studied Joanna a moment. "This disguise is very clever, but you really need something better for the auction. Oh, I know." Luna snapped her fingers. "I've got just the thing."

She lifted a hatbox from beside her desk and handed it to Joanna. Inside was a shoulder-length black wig styled in a smooth pageboy. Joanna grinned. "Not the Cleopatra."

Luna laughed. "Guaranteed to make you not look like Joanna Edwards."

A knock at the shop door startled them all. Luna hastened to her office door and peered out. "Oh my God. It's that nosy cop. Go out the back door and down the alley. Quickly."

Cade opened the back door of the Galleria and scanned the alley in both directions. Dumpsters blocked the view, but as well as he could tell, no one was watching it. They hurried to the end of the building, the rush of road and sidewalk traffic growing louder as they neared the main street.

Cody found the brisk pace delightful. His laugh punctuated Joanna's racing heartbeat. For all that was wrong with her world at the moment, this one thing was wholly right. Despite the fear flowing through her, she grabbed on to that feeling, touched her son's cheek and thanked God for him.

And for Cade.

A Tukwila Police Department vehicle was parked outside the Galleria. Luna had the police detective inside. Cade caught Joanna's elbow, leaned close enough that his warm breath filtered through the hat brim. "That's O'Brien, one of the men who was at my house yesterday. If he sees me, no telling what he'll do. What he'll think. You cross the street ahead of me—like we're not together. Go into that travel agency by the SUV and watch out the window. If he catches sight of me, I'll tell him I'm doing some private investigating on my own."

One of the disadvantages of being six foot four was being unable to blend in a crowd.

"Will he believe that?" she whispered.

"Probably. Anyway, if you see me leave, don't

panic. I'll circle the block, make sure O'Brien isn't following me and come back and pick you up.''

''Okay.'' Joanna skipped past Cade.

He slowed down, letting a few feet separate them, then a yard, two. She could hear Cody chattering and moved with speed into the center of the road, crossing on the Walk light.

She heard the revving engine before the danger registered.

Out of the corner of her eye, Joanna spied a black sedan leaping over the median. It charged toward the intersection. Fast. Faster. Coming straight for her.

Chapter Eleven

Joanna leaped back. The charging car adjusted, re-aligning to hit her head-on. She heard a man shout. Felt herself being shoved out of harm's way. Knocked off balance. The hatbox kept her face from hitting the pavement. But not her knees or hands. Pain radiated from the scraped skin. The hatbox punched her rib cage. Air whooshed from her lungs. Behind her, she heard a loud thud. Another scream. A thump. Tires squealing. A hard breeze whipped past, inches from her backside.

The air went still, the brilliant day dulled, the silence was consuming as though all motion, all sound, all life had ceased, only to come alive seconds later with a burst of noise and voices and vivid terror.

"Cody. Cade." Joanna thrashed around, her cries lost in the riot of shouts and crunch of bodies rushing into the street, running to the aid of the man sprawled on the pavement. *Cade?* Terror strangled her. "Cody. Cade."

She levered her weight on the dented hatbox, but before she could pull herself up, she felt strong hands grip her upper arms. A second later Cade was crushing her to him. "Are you all right?"

She threw her arms around him, hugging him, touching her son, absorbing the fact that the three of them were alive. Unharmed. Tears burned her eyes, and hysterical laughter bubbled from her throat. "Oh, God, I thought that was you behind me. I thought the car hit you and...and Cody."

They were alive. *They were alive.* She wanted to shout it. But it struck her then that someone hadn't been as lucky as they, and her joyous relief dissolved to horror. She twisted from his embrace and covered her mouth with her hands. "Oh no, Cade. Who is that in the street? Is he—?"

"I don't know. But we can't stick around and find out." Cade spoke in a desperate whisper. "O'Brien is there. Investigating. Someone is bound to tell him that you were the target of that hit-and-run. He'll want to talk to you. We have to leave. Now."

"But that man saved my life. We—"

Cade had one arm around her. He snatched up the hatbox as they passed it, steadily steering Joanna toward the SUV. "Do you want to make his sacrifice for nothing?"

"No." She moved by rote. Urged on as much by Cade as Cody. The baby was crying. The noise and excitement, Cade's and her distress were all too much for him.

At the SUV, she lifted Cody from the backpack, cuddled him, comforted him, thanked God he was unharmed, perfect, wonderful, hers. She strapped him into the car seat, and settled beside him as Cade, in front, started the engine. Her gentle whispers soon calmed Cody, and she was rewarded with a teary smile. He accepted his bottle.

Cade inched the SUV slowly through the crowded

street. As they came to the corner, he spotted O'Brien.
The Tukwila police officer spun toward the SUV, the
movement swift as though he was responding to some
inner voice that had told him to look at the SUV at
that particular moment. Cade's and his gazes locked,
for just a second.

Cade saw recognition, surprise and curiosity register
in rapid succession on O'Brien's dark face. Cade's
belly clutched. He broke eye contact and pressed his
foot harder on the gas pedal, whipping around a corner
and out of sight. But had he moved quickly enough?
Or had O'Brien noticed the woman with Cody?

Cade glanced at Joanna in the rearview mirror.
She'd pulled off the hat, undone her hair; it fell soft
around her shoulders, lovely, shiny, exactly the style
in the photo being shown on every news report and
paper in the Northwest.

She hadn't even realized she'd abandoned the disguise that was protecting her. It hadn't occurred to her.
Her first concern was Cody. Running on shock, he
figured.

He doubted anyone could have seen her well
enough to identify her, after all the SUV windows
were dark. But if O'Brien decided to follow them?
Stopped them? He gazed beyond Joanna, checking for
that Tukwila sedan in the sea of traffic behind them.
Was one of those dark cars O'Brien's? The knot in
his gut tightened. They needed to get out of sight,
pronto.

No. He had to quit panic-thinking. He gave himself
a mental slap, drew a deep breath and released it to a
count of ten, an exercise he'd learned at the academy.
O'Brien wouldn't have made it back to his car and
through that crowd fast enough to tail them. If the

officer had done anything, he'd have alerted every cop in Seattle to be on the lookout for this vehicle.

THE SWAY of the SUV began to lull Cody, to ease him into a gentle sleep. With her son calmed, Joanna felt her shock retreat. Only then did she notice the burning pain in her knees and the heels of her hands. There was blood on her borrowed dress. Her blood? Or that of the man in the street?

Tremors rippled through her. "They meant to kill me."

Cade found an alley and parked. He got out and into the back seat with her. He opened his arms and Joanna huddled into him, quaking, crying, her sobs and her tears absorbed by his jacket, his wonderfully strong and steadying embrace. She had no idea how long she cried. But not long. These weren't tears of grief or self-pity, but those of shock and horror.

When the tears were spent, she lifted her head and gazed up at Cade. "Thank you."

He smiled as if to say no big deal and daubed smeared makeup from beneath her eyes with his hankie. "Your hands and knees are bleeding. There's a first-aid kit under the passenger seat." He moved to retrieve it.

She caught his arm. "Cade, that car...someone meant to kill me."

He pulled the metal first-aid kit onto his lap and nodded. "I figure we were IDed at the hotel." He opened the kit and gathered some hydrogen peroxide, bandages and antiseptic cream. He moistened a cotton swab with peroxide. "It's the only explanation."

"Then someone knows we're together." She winced as he cleaned her wounds, the sting equaling the pain in her heart at the realization that her desire to stay with her son was selfish, foolish and deadly. "I'll have to leave you and Cody. I won't risk either of your lives like this again." Her mind flashed to the man who'd been lying in the street. "My God, if you'd been behind me, you and Cody—"

She couldn't even say the awful thing out loud.

"Cody and I are fine and I intend to keep it that way." Cade spread antiseptic on one knee, then the other, his fingers warm and sure, his touch gentle. He secured the bandages. "But you are not taking off. Not now. We're going to your studio and collect some of your paintings for that auction. No. Don't argue. Getting inside the Addison mansion is our only hope of finding some evidence to prove you didn't kill Nan."

He kissed her then, his mouth as sweet a retreat as she'd ever known. The last of the tension slipped from her body as desire came alive in her. She felt his hands in her hair, on her back, through her dress, and a delicious heat swept her blood.

Too soon, he pulled away. His words were breathy. "I'd really like the time to explore this, but I'm afraid O'Brien may still be lurking. We have to get moving."

He touched her hair. Her loose hair. The hat? She spied it tossed in the back of the vehicle. When had she removed it? Pulled out the hairpins? She retraced the moments after the hit-and-run, her own actions, and realized they'd still been at the accident scene. "Dear God. Did O'Brien see me?"

"I don't know. If he did, it wasn't well enough to identify you, or we'd be surrounded by SPD right this minute."

She blanched. "Guess I'll be using that black wig sooner than expected—like now."

"Not a bad idea," he concurred. "We need to get out of here."

She plucked the wig from the crumpled hatbox. It was mussed but undamaged. She twisted her own hair and pinned it to her head, then pulled on the wig. "What do you think?"

"It's kind of sexy." Cade smiled. "But there are a few blond wisps sticking out. You'd better use the visor mirror."

They got into the front seat, and Cade concentrated on driving as she adjusted the wig.

They gained the freeway out of Seattle without being stopped. Cade relaxed slightly, but scanned the mirrors and kept alert. "We're going to Spokane. Tonight. Right now, however, we're going back to the lake house, trade my SUV for Lynne's SUV—since it's untraceable—shower, change, take naps, load up baby supplies and whatever else we might need. As soon as it's dusk, we'll hit the road again."

EVEN AT one in the morning, I-90 through Spokane was heavily traveled. Businesses and hospitals lined up along both sides of the freeway, easily accessible. The city was large, reaching its arms of growth northward to the Canadian border and eastward toward Idaho, spreading in all directions to accommodate the ever-increasing population.

"Which exit did you say?" Cade asked, his hands taut on the steering wheel. He recalled only that he'd associated the exit she'd mentioned with an old television variety show. But he was tired from six hours of driving; his brain needed fresh air, his cramped muscles stretching.

"Sullivan," she said. "It's one of the last before the Idaho border."

Silence ensued, and Cade spent the next few miles considering what might greet them at the home Joanna had shared with her father. "Your house is probably being watched."

She tried to laugh, but it came out grim, a bark of despair. "By the police *and* Addison's thugs."

"Any suggestions on how a woman and man with a baby in tow are going to ford the guarded citadel and gain the coveted treasures?"

"Now *that* is a better question than you might imagine. When the attacks began, my father had a fence put around the perimeter of our half acre, then had a silent alarm security system installed. But fences can be breached and wires disconnected or cut."

"And were they?"

"Yes. One night a bomb went off in the garbage can behind the house. Damage was minimal. It was a warning, something to show us that we weren't safe no matter what we did. After that, Dad planted his own set of booby traps. The backyard is like a minefield. If we hit one of those trip wires, all hell will erupt."

"You don't know where the trip wires are?"

"Not a clue. And besides that, I no longer have the keys to my house or my studio. They were on my car-key ring."

He glanced sharply at her, not liking the drift of this conversation. "Obtaining some of your paintings is getting more difficult by the minute."

"Can't you pick the lock?"

"I'm a cop not a cat burglar."

"Does that mean no?"

"No." To catch thieves, more often than not, he'd had to become one.

"If you're not comfortable with that, maybe I can get a key from...one of my neighbors."

"Oh, you have a neighbor who doesn't read or watch TV?"

His words were like ice water on her tired brain. She kept forgetting she was a suspect in a murder case, being sought in a statewide hunt. If Cade were seen with her, his career would be over. As an officer of the court he was already in big trouble, but if they were both arrested Cody would be placed in county care, as Cade had been from birth on. The thought made her sick to her stomach.

"Bob won't—"

"Bob?" He heard her exhale.

She said, "My ex-fiancé. He lives next door and has a key to my house."

Her ex-fiancé? The man she'd nearly married two weeks ago? He *still* had a key to her house? Why? Did she still love him? Was there a possibility when this mess was over that she'd get back together with Bob?

There was an odd twinge in Cade's throat, in his chest. Recall filled his mind with the memory of her mouth sweet and hot on his, and he discovered to his deep surprise that he couldn't bear it if she realized any time soon that she should never have broken it off with this...Bob guy. "Was your breakup amicable?"

"No." Her voice was laced with guilt. "But it was inevitable. The best thing for both of us."

Cade suddenly felt sorry for the man who'd loved and lost this woman. He glanced at her. "Why does he *still* have a key to your house?"

"I forgot to get it back." In the glow of the dashboard he saw her shift in her seat. "Bob is a wonderful guy and I really hurt him. We've been friends since we were kids. We should never have been anything more. He imagines he's in love with me. I've never been in love with him, though I do love him as a friend."

The strange tightness in Cade's chest eased. He had no right to ask the question he was about to, but he had to know. He kept his voice as gentle as the night. "How did you end up almost walking down the aisle with this guy, then?"

As they drove along the Sullivan off-ramp, she said, "Bob was so good to me during my pregnancy, through the attempts to murder my father and me, and after I *lost* my baby. I mistook gratitude for obligation."

"You thought you'd pay back his kindnesses by becoming his wife?" He said this gently, sympathetically, secretly relieved that Bob hadn't been the love of her life. That that position might still be open, waiting for the right candidate to fill it. Was *he* that candidate? Did he want to be?

"I know it was crazy. But I didn't realize it at the time. Bob wanted our relationship to go to the next level and I knew he was losing patience. I couldn't bear to lose him, to have his support removed, so I agreed to marry him."

Cade glanced at the crowded parking lots of the hotels on both sides of the road as they passed. "Marriages have been undertaken for worse reasons."

"I guess. Anyway, Dad's death and finding out my baby was alive shocked me out of the zombie existence I'd retreated to. But there was no way to avoid hurting Bob.''

Cade laid his hand over hers and squeezed, hoping his touch conveyed sympathy and understanding. ''Sometimes doing the right thing is the hardest thing of all.''

He felt her fingers flinch beneath his and wondered why.

She said, ''He didn't take it well. He was very angry.''

Cade thought about that a moment, about how he'd feel if he'd been told the woman he planned to marry had never loved him. ''Under the circumstances Bob could be a danger to us.''

''You think he'll alert the police if he spots us?''

''Don't you?''

She was quiet as they waited for the stoplight to turn green. ''Maybe. Probably. At the least, he'd try to talk me into turning myself in.''

Cade lifted his foot from the brake to the gas pedal. They were heading south, past small strip malls. ''How much farther?''

''We'll be going all the way to East Belle Terre Avenue and turning right.'' She pulled down the visor and checked the wig in the lighted mirror. Cade could see her face was pale, her eyes overly bright in the dim yellow light. She snapped the mirror shut and glanced at him. ''Hopefully, Bob will be in bed when we arrive. He retires every night at nine.''

''A man of rigid routine.'' The more he learned about her ex-fiancé, the happier he was that she'd broken it off with him. He sounded like the kind of guy who scheduled sex by the calendar. Cade couldn't say why, but he sensed Joanna flourished on diversity, that she would feel trapped in any kind of regimented life-style.

"Bob runs a garbage disposal service. He starts work before most of us are out of bed."

"Let's pray he sticks to his routine tonight." Spotting a road sign with East Belle Terre Ave on it, Cade slowed and turned right. There was little traffic on the road now.

They rode in silence for a few miles, then she told him to slow and take a left. "On East Forty-second Avenue, take a right. It's the middle house in the cul-de-sac."

Cade pulled to the curb one house away from Joanna's. He scanned the neighborhood, surveillance being one of his specialities. He liked knowing the lay of the land before going into any war zone. Most of the lights were out in the houses on either side of the street. Except for the occasional bark of a dog, and the lamplights overhead, the night was still.

As far as he could tell, of the cars parked on the road, none were occupied. Neither police nor anyone else seemed to be watching the Edwards's house. His gut twitched. Something he couldn't see, couldn't define brushed like a wet feather across the nape of his neck, sending a shiver down his spine. "Which house is Bob's?"

"The blue one. On the right." She glanced at the house as she pointed to it. There was a light on in a back room. His bedroom. "That's odd."

"What?" Cade's grip tightened on the steering wheel.

"Bob's bedroom light is on. He never gets up in the middle of the night. He's a sound sleeper."

"How sound?"

"That bomb in our garbage can? He slept right through it."

"Well, his life has been turned upside down the last two weeks. Maybe he's suffering a bout of insomnia."

"Thanks. I don't feel guilty enough as it is."

"Sorry." Cade prayed Bob wasn't, at this moment, spying on them.

She said, "I hate to disturb Cody, he's sleeping so peacefully. Maybe you should stay here while I collect the paintings."

"No. Cody will keep on sleeping." Cade was out of the vehicle and had Cody in the backpack within seconds. He handed Joanna a flashlight, then closed his doors quietly, signaling for her to do the same. "Besides, you need someone to pick the lock, remember?"

Scanning the neighborhood in both directions, they walked gingerly to her front gate. He sniffed, then asked in a whisper, "Do you smell smoke?"

"Yes," she whispered in answer.

"Who'd be burning wood this time of year?"

She shrugged. "Don't know. I hope no one's changed my security code."

"We don't need to worry about that." Cade shone the flashlight on a box on the fence. The wires of her alarm system had been ripped out. Likely the security company had tried contacting her, but of course, she couldn't be found. Even in the dim illumination he could see her fury.

Cade eased the gate open and they hurried to the stoop. In the moonlight, the house appeared to be a gray rambler with white window boxes and gingerbread trim. Here, too, the wires had been wrenched from the security box.

Cade shone the light on the doorknob. There were no telltale signs of tampering. He tested it and was not surprised to find that it turned easily in his hand. The door swung inward. The bad feeling he'd had earlier returned in spades. "I want you to take Cody and go back to Lynne's SUV."

"No. We're staying with you."

"Someone might be inside waiting with an unpleasant surprise."

"We're safer with you than without you."

"That's crazy."

"Is it? You've got the gun. You know how to use it. What chance will we have if someone corners us outside and you're in here?"

Cade swore, but consented. He unstrapped the backpack. Cody stirred, his heavy eyes slitting, then closing again as Joanna took him. "We'll stay in the living room," she promised.

"Stay here until I tell you it's safe to come inside. But if you hear me yell to get out, do it. Fast." He gave her the keys to their vehicle.

"Okay," she whispered.

He came back a second later. "All clear."

She slipped into the foyer, retrieved a flashlight from the entry closet and used it to find her way in the darkened living room, taking a position against the fireplace.

As soon as he knew she and Cody were tucked out of sight, he took the safety off his Glock and with the barrel pointing to the floor, the flashlight in the other hand, he inched along the hallway.

He came to a door. Shoved it inward. Panned the light beam over the walls. A bathroom. Neat. Empty. No one lurking behind the shower curtain. He crept to the next room. A bedroom. Then another. And another. No one was in this part of the house.

His pulse kicked. The bad feeling growing stronger instead of weaker. He strained to detect any unwelcome noises in any other part of the house as he hurried back into the hall. At the bathroom, he turned left, reached through the doorway and ended up in the kitchen. Once again, he splayed the light over the room. No one was hiding in any corner.

He blew out his breath, relief easing the band around his chest. Then his light picked up something that caused his heart to leap: a plate-size, crimson pool on the floor beneath the dishwasher.

Moving gingerly, he crossed to it, bent, poked a finger in the gooey puddle and sniffed, wincing at the tinny acrid odor. As he'd suspected. Blood. His gut flipped. He swore. Rusty-colored droplets led like spilled paint across to the far wall and out the back door, which stood ajar.

Behind him, he heard Joanna gasp. He rounded on her. "I told you to stay put."

"Is that blood?" Her eyes were wide with horror and fear, her face ashen against the black wig. "What's that?"

She was pointing to something near the pool of blood, shining her flashlight beam on it.

Cade saw it then, amazed that he'd missed it the first time. A button. It was large and ornate with some kind of design embossed on it. It was unusual. One of a kind? Handmade, maybe? Who could afford to have buttons handmade?

Joanna crossed to it, squatted, and reached to pick it up.

"No!" Cade warned. "Don't touch anything!"

He caught her by the elbow. "Go back to the car. Now. I'll get the paintings and meet you there."

Watching where he stepped, he moved to the back door. He heard Joanna right behind him. He turned to her. "What are you doing?"

She hugged Cody to her, her chin set at a stubborn angle. "You won't know which paintings to bring or where the traveling case is. It will be faster if I come with you."

Despite his every misgiving, he relented. They exited into a wide backyard. "Stay on the stepping stones," Joanna advised. "And you won't hit any of Dad's 'land mines.'"

Somewhere nearby, the sound of police sirens rent the air.

The studio skylights were bright with an eerie wavering orange light. The stench of smoke was strong.

It took Cade a moment to put the two things together. He grabbed Joanna, stopping her in her tracks. A stifled cry leaped from her. "My paintings."

There was no mistaking what they were looking at. The studio was on fire.

Chapter Twelve

"My paintings!" Joanna screamed. "No!" She thrust Cody at Cade. He grabbed his son awkwardly in one arm as she lurched toward the burning building.

"No!" Cade lunged for her, clamping his hand around her upper arm and stopping her in her tracks. It was like trying to hold on to a fleeing gang member. "No, Joanna! No! You can't! It's too late. It's too late. The fire's too intense. The paintings are lost."

Shaking her head in denial, she kept struggling, trying to shake him off. Her sobs rivaled the crackle of the flames licking across canvas and wood, the occasional explosion as fire touched paint and thinner.

Hugging Cody to him, Cade dug his fingers into Joanna's arm, sure he was hurting her, hoping if he was that the pain would penetrate her frenzied mind. She wrenched harder against his hold. He jerked her around, yanking her close to him until he had her face inches from his own. Her eyes were wide, but he finally had her attention. He spoke each word individually. "It's. Too. Late."

She blinked and shuddered out a heavy breath. She glanced toward Cody, then back up at Cade. She shut her eyes, shook her head and sucked in a sob. "No...I...it's...it..."

The fight went out of her. He released her. This time she stayed put. He skimmed his knuckles along the curve of her cheek. "I'm sorry."

She moaned, nuzzling his fingers, then pressing her other cheek against Cody's small head. Cade circled her shoulders with his free arm, embracing these two precious people to his heart, the hug awkward despite how right it felt. He spoke gently, "You aren't alone. Cody and I are on your side."

She glanced up at him again, but he couldn't tell if he was getting through to her. The heat from the fire scented the night air and he knew the risk of standing so near the studio. The windows might burst at any moment. Cade drew her back a few steps, then a few more. In the distance he heard a sound that made him feel as though a sharp nail had been scraped up his spine, as though everything was suddenly clearer, more acutely focused.

Danger more imminent.

Dear God, the sirens he'd noticed earlier. They were coming closer. "Joanna, we have to get out of here."

He shifted Cody in his arm, gripping him more securely, then gathered Joanna's hand in his and held tightly. He pulled her around the side of the house, keeping to the stepping stones, and out through the fence. She stumbled along beside him, her resistence minimal. If one of the neighbors had called the fire department it was more than likely they'd be outside to welcome their arrival.

The street was deserted, the neighborhood still, as though no one were aware of the threat to their homes.

No one was coming to put out the fire. Those sirens

had to belong to the police. He jerked around, looking up and down the street again. Was whoever had called the cops there yet? Did someone besides the gallery owner know they were in Spokane? That they would be coming to the house? He gritted his teeth. Either he and Joanna had incredibly bad timing, or a 911 call had been timed in order to catch them here. If so, why? Cade swore, understanding instantly. The blood in Joanna's kitchen, of course.

So much blood.

Whose blood?

Where was the body?

He glanced back at the burning building and shuddered. God, let him move quickly enough to get Joanna and Cody safely away.

"Wait." Joanna cried. "I'll be right back."

"No. We can't stay."

"But there are a couple of my watercolors on the living-room wall."

"No. The police are coming. They'll be here in seconds. We can't risk it."

"But if the house catches fire…"

He handed her Cody and shoved them both into the front seat. The diversion worked. She stopped protesting and hooked her seat belt. He figured the baby would be safe enough in her arms until they were out of this neighborhood. He pushed her door shut, then raced to his side of the vehicle and leaped inside. Leaving the lights off, he drove out to the main street, then turned right and right again onto Forty-third Avenue.

He made a U-turn there and parked at the stop sign. Four seconds later two police cars, sirens silent, lights flashing, barreled toward them, then careened onto Forty-second Avenue. Joanna's street.

Cade waited until the taillights disappeared and stepped on the gas. Minutes later, they were back on East Belle Terre Avenue. He turned on the SUV lights. No one was speeding up from behind them. In fact, no one was behind them.

He released a sigh.

But Joanna was still holding herself stiff. In the light from the dash, she looked stunned. She'd said nothing. She just held to Cody as if he was the only thing left in her life, as though this tiny being was the only source of comfort in a world blown to hell.

Cade knew that feeling. Something about holding his son made the craziness seem less so. "I'm going to get us a motel room. Just down the road here."

She said nothing, just kissed Cody's head and closed her eyes. He reached over and stroked his sleeping son's hair, his cheek, Joanna's cheek.

Joanna peered at him with wide, unseeing eyes. He imagined her mind was still on the studio. He couldn't even guess how she had to be feeling. She'd lost her father, her baby, and now her life's work, and if the fire should leap from the studio to her house, she would likely lose her every worldly possession. But even then, it wasn't all that pressed her heart. She was wanted for a murder she hadn't committed. She'd lost her freedom; she could lose her life.

Cade reached across the seat and caught her hand in his. It felt small and icy. "I'm sorry."

That sounded so lame, but it was all he had to offer.

She gave him a wobbly smile and spoke in a tiny voice, "Why would Shane destroy my work? What could he possibly hope to gain? It's not like I'm supporting myself with my art. The two paintings Luna just sold are the first two I've ever earned money for.''

''I don't know.'' Cade shook his head. It hadn't occurred to her to ask whose blood was on her kitchen floor. But he knew it would penetrate sooner or later…when the shock of the fire wore off.

She began to shiver and Cade knew he had to get her someplace quiet, somewhere she could vent this grief and rage.

He pulled into the Red Lion Inn. He liked the fact that the ground-floor rooms had sliding glass doors out to the parking lot. It would allow them an escape route, if necessary.

He got a room with two beds and toted the baby's gear in, letting her carry Cody. Her face was so pale against the raven-colored wig, it scared him.

She insisted on settling Cody into his travel bed, putting him down carefully, her manner tender and motherly. He was touched by her concern for his son. But she needed the same attention.

''You smell smoky. We're going to have to air out that wig.'' He caught her gently by the shoulders and guided her to the bed nearest the door. She was as pliant as a child, as vulnerable, as innocent. He began undoing the wig. Taking out the hairpins that anchored it to her head. He loosened her own hair, her glorious caramel hair.

It fell about her shoulders like a shimmering wave of silk. He touched the strands, then thrust his fingers into the velvety tresses, massaging her scalp, lifting a floral fragrance like rosebuds in spring. The scent got inside him, churned his blood, made it throb hot and bold through his veins, filled him with a need that was at once familiar, and yet, singular, original, unique. Something he'd never experienced.

But she needed something different from him at the moment. He pulled her into his arms. She clung to him as she'd been clinging to Cody earlier, as though he were the only barrier between sanity and complete madness.

JOANNA'S INSIDES felt stony, concrete heavy. Her studio was gone. Except for the few paintings she'd given friends and the older watercolors in her house, all of her work, gone. "Will the house burn, too?"

"I don't know. Probably not." He stroked her hair, his touch gentle, comforting, and she sensed he was telling her what she wanted to hear, only what he thought she could deal with. His kindness gave her heart. He said, "The police are there. They'll call the fire department."

"Yes. Yes. The house will be fine. The police will—" She stared at the buttons on Cade's denim shirt, and saw another button, a blood-soaked button. She sat straighter. Stiffened. Looking at him then. Frowning. "They'll find the blood. All that blood. How could anyone live after losing so much blood?" Her glance sharpened. "Whose blood is it, Cade?"

He shook his head. "I don't know."

"You didn't find a body in the house?"

"No."

"Outside?"

"No."

"The studio...?"

He shrugged. "I guess we'll know soon enough."

She wrapped her arms around her middle, but couldn't hide the tremors wracking her body. "Who would have been in my house? The front door didn't look forced open, did it?''

''No.'' He was cautious, holding back, not asking her the obvious.

''Bob and my cousin Kenner are the only two who have keys, the only two who knew the security code.''

He said, ''It's not likely that either of them would have ripped out the wires to the security system, then.''

''No. But what if one of them was inside the house when the person who did rip out the wires came calling?'' She trembled harder at this possibility. ''What if one of them was attacked? K-killed?''

Cade's arms swept around her, those big strong arms that formed a haven, a retreat from all that horror and terror. Joanna took refuge there for long minutes. But she couldn't shake off the cold that seemed to have permeated every cell in her body and burned like dry ice in her brain.

She wedged her hands against his chest, pushed up and away from him, the panic gripping her anew. ''We have to call them. I have to know that they're okay. I can't lose anyone else. I can't.''

She pounced for the phone. Cade grabbed her wrist, stopping her. ''No. Use the cell phone. We don't want anyone tracing our whereabouts. We can't risk that either of their phones isn't being monitored by the police.''

He handed her the cell phone, but she was trembling too much to dial. She told him the phone numbers. He dialed Bob Massey first. After ten rings, he disconnected. ''No answer.''

She couldn't think about the light on in Bob's bedroom and the fact that his answering machine wasn't on without being afraid for him. "Where is he?"

Cade pressed his lips together and touched her shoulder. "We shouldn't jump to the conclusion that the blood is Bob's. He might be spending the night elsewhere."

"Elsewhere?"

"Well, yeah. You did just break up with him. Maybe he's out. Or...something."

Out? She hadn't thought of that. It was possible. She embraced the suggestion. Finding hope in it. "Try Kenner."

She gave him the number, and Cade dialed. After a minute, he disconnected. "Either he's a heavy sleeper or he's not there."

Joanna hugged herself tighter, bending over. It didn't help that she could still smell the smoke from the fire. It was on her clothes as well as seared into her olfactory memory.

Cade had his hankie out. He wiped at a spot on her face. "Soot," he answered her querulous expression. "Maybe a hot bath or shower would make you feel better."

She nodded, numbly rising. She'd showered earlier at the lake house, but now she felt dirty, her body stiff and sore, the cold all-consuming.

She went first to Cody. He was sleeping with his little bottom in the air. She stroked his silken neck, tucked the blanket over him, then crossed to the bathroom. She turned on the water in the tub/shower combination, stripped and stepped beneath the hot shower, its jet force beating on her goose-bumped flesh.

Her mind felt violated, as though the arsonist had reached into her head and struck a match to her visions. She could paint again. She *would* paint again. But she could never retrieve the paintings he'd destroyed. Each one had been like a piece of who she was and what she was dealing with at the time they'd been created.

Selling the paintings gave her a similar sense of loss, but sold paintings existed. Somewhere. Knowing they were out there in the world gave her a sense of security, a sense of herself that nothing else had.

But destroyed... This loss felt like another death.

Pain swelled in her chest. Tears flooded her eyes. She sank to her haunches and began sobbing uncontrollably, letting out excess pressure, tapping the release valve to avoid an emotional implosion.

Cade came to her, whipped aside the shower curtain, stepped into the shower, lifted her up against him. He was barefoot, but still wore a T-shirt and jeans. He was oblivious to the water drenching his clothes.

She lifted her arms around his neck, clinging to him, needing him now for more than support, more than comfort, needing him as a man, needing him to make her feel like a woman, needing him to make her feel alive. She welcomed his lips on hers with a raging desperation, but was more desperate still to feel his naked flesh against hers.

She snagged the hem of his T-shirt, pulling it up and over his head, breaking the kiss only until the shirt was no longer a barrier between their hungry mouths. Greedily, she slicked her hands up his flat, wet belly, felt his nipples harden, felt her own respond in kind.

Desire roared through her, chasing the chill from her blood, replacing it with something electrifying, something dizzying, something she'd never experienced until *this* moment, with *this* man. She reached for the waistband of his jeans and found his hands already there. Together they stripped off his pants and tossed the wet clothes out onto the floor.

He was sleek and lean and hard in all the right places; her fingers couldn't get enough of the feel of him. His tongue parted her lips, darting in and out, stroking, delving, tasting, speeding passion through her with the recklessness and rapture of a tropical rain, searing her with white-hot cravings.

She laced her fingers through his thick hair, pulling him closer, cherishing the feel of his mouth on hers, his tongue twined with hers dancing a tune of their own, this pleasure exquisite. "Oh, Cade," she said on a breathless sigh. "Don't stop, please, don't stop."

He groaned and his hands began to rove her backside from shoulder to bottom, and up again, then down again. Desire sluiced through her, a need as ripe as summer, as crisp as autumn, as new as spring, as wet as winter. She ached to have him inside her, needed him there, needed to feel that honeyed friction, that life-creating blend of male and female joining, needed to lose herself in that ultimate form of ecstasy, needed affirmation that despite everything she'd lost, she had not lost herself.

He pulled back, breaking the kiss, his hands slicking down her arms, his gaze slipping over her body, awe in the depths of his glorious eyes. "Joanna, my Joanna. Where have you been all of my life?"

There was such guileless wonder in his question, such heartfelt honesty, she knew he meant it. This was no line. He apparently felt what she was feeling at the moment: as though she'd known him in another time or place, as though she'd been searching all of this life for him and him alone, as though this was destined long before either had known of the other.

He grazed his knuckles across her breasts as gently as a brush stroke, his tenderness seductive, sensuous, sending tingles to her very core. A smile filled his eyes, curved his mouth. She laughed with joy and welcomed his kiss that skimmed her lips, her jaw, her neck, the hollow of her throat, and lower, until finally, his tongue found and flicked across her right nipple, then the left, leaving each stiffened to crystal buds. He suckled one, taking it deep into his hot mouth, then the other, switching back and forth, again and again.

She moaned in sweet agony, feeling attacked from within, her belly and lower awash in want, her breasts and higher assaulted with bliss, her mind and spirit mesmerized by Cade Maconahey. She returned his erotic attack, tracing her hands over his tight behind, up his narrow waist to the broad width of his back, then circling to his chest. She teased her fingers through the patch of hair between his taut nipples, then dragged her hands slowly down his washboard belly and lower into the denser hair at his groin.

"Oh, Joanna. Oh." He groaned and threw back his head as she cupped him with one hand, then grasped his throbbing erection with the other. Again he cried out her name, the sound so soft and sweet it might be a song of love. Water from the shower spigot rippled over them, a waterfall against her hair, down her face.

She moved her hand over the length of his penis; it felt as sleek and satiny as silk, the tip rounded and turgid, damp and tantalizing, irresistible. Fascinated by this new appreciation of the male anatomy, she fondled him, tasted him, brought him fully into her mouth and pleasured him until his fingers dug deep into her shoulders and he pulled her back up the length of him.

He kissed her again, his hands on each side of her face, then he pulled her to him, slipping his hand between them, moving it to the hottest part of her body, his fingers probing her, eliciting a quick slamming climax that startled them both.

He raised her arms to his shoulders, then lifted her. Locking her hands about his neck, she wrapped her legs around his hips, then lowered herself onto him. He was hard and thick and filled her as though they'd been fashioned one for the other.

She gazed into his cerulean eyes, the blue dark with ardor, warm with pleasure, the same pleasure she imagined as was coursing through her. He began to move, pushing in and out of her, the movements slow and deep, then quick and quicker. Every thrust was more exquisite than the last, spiraling her higher and higher into a land of enchantment she'd only read about, had heard existed but never visited before this night.

She closed her eyes and stars flashed against the blackness, fire bursts of delirium that cascaded time and again from the roots of her hair to her fingertips and toes. "Cade. Oh, yes, Cade. Yes, yes, yes!"

He answered with a shout of his own, his body tensing with release, a hot rush of liquid flooding into her, filling her with pure bliss. She clutched his neck, kissing him, then raising her face and staring deep into his eyes, the eyes of the man who had just captured her heart.

The need she'd seen, almost from the first, in those wonderful eyes of his had changed, evolved. He was looking at her as though he'd discovered the home he'd never had, never known growing up. He made no move to separate from her, and she felt him growing hard again inside her.

She sighed sensuously, meeting his gaze, fearing in that moment that she was staring into the face of the man she could be falling in love with. A man who had, in a few short days, made her happier than she'd been in years, than she had a right to be at the moment. A man whose heart she would soon break.

But now was not the time to think of that.

They made love again.

Afterward, they bathed each other, dried each other, fussed over Cody, then dropped into bed and made love once more. Joanna fell asleep in Cade's arms, too content, too exhausted to wonder about the blood in her kitchen, to contemplate what horror the morning would bring.

A few miles away, a crew of firefighters had doused the flames in her studio. Among the ashes, they had discovered a body.

Chapter Thirteen

"Should we order breakfast in bed?" Cade woke her with a kiss behind her ear.

Joanna smiled and pried her eyes open. "What time is it?"

Cade rolled away from her and glanced at the clock. "Make that brunch. It's almost eleven."

"Cody." Joanna jerked upright in bed, immediately concerned as to why the baby hadn't awakened them before now. But she needn't have worried. Cody was sitting up, playing with his bunny, chewing on one of its terry-cloth ears.

He seemed to intuit her attention and his head lifted, his gaze locking with hers. He dropped the bunny and stretched his tiny arms toward her, babbling, "Ma-mamamamamama."

Joanna's heart swelled. She threw back the covers and began to rise.

"Oh no you don't," Cade teased, catching her by the wrist and pulling her back down beside him, nuzzling her neck. "I need you here."

Joanna raised herself on an elbow and looked from one to the other of them. "You're a demanding pair of males, aren't you?"

Cody jabbered louder, his hopeful expression crumbling, his chatter taking on a whining tone. Cade laughed and released her. "It seems my son thinks he's the dominant male in this household. When he's a little older, I'll set him straight on that point."

Cade grabbed pillows, plunked them behind his head and picked up the TV remote. He began scanning channels.

Joanna went to her son and lifted him to her thundering heart. At this moment, she felt as light as tracing paper, a content feeling she usually only experienced when one of her paintings was going well.

The thought snatched the pleasant feelings, conjuring horrid images of the night before: the blood in her kitchen, her studio burning. At the same moment, Cade stopped channel surfing on a local news broadcast. Joanna twisted toward the TV, automatically gripping Cody tighter. There was a photograph inset above the anchorman's head, first of her house, then of her face, then Bob's face.

"Turn it up," she told Cade, stumbling to the bed.

He obliged, and the newscaster's voice cut through her like jagged glass. "Early this morning, a fire was reported at the home of Joanna Edwards, the woman being sought for questioning in the death of an Issaquah midwife. The fire was contained to an artist studio behind the house. After putting out the two-alarm blaze, the fire department discovered the charred remains of Ms. Edwards's neighbor and former fiancé, Bob Massey, the owner of a local garbage disposal company."

"Bob!" Joanna cried. "No!"

Startled, Cody began to cry. Cade leaped from beneath the covers and reached for Joanna. She shook her head, pressed Cody into his arms and gagged. She covered her mouth with her hand, ran into the bathroom, and was sick. Dry heaves wracked her until her stomach felt turned inside out.

Afterward, she sank to the floor, clammy, shivering. Her eyes burned, but tears refused to come, dammed behind a barrier of shock and grief. She sat, hugging her knees to her chest for long minutes. Eventually, she struggled to her feet.

She wiped her face with a cool cloth and rinsed out her mouth. Her complexion was ashen in the mirror, dark smudges underscored each eye, her mouth was tight, the flesh white at the corners. As she stared at herself, her image faded, replaced by Bob's, not as she'd just seen on television, but the last time she'd seen him. Angry. Hurt.

Just three days ago. Now he was dead. Why? Had he surprised the person who'd broken into her house? Been killed in an accidental encounter because she'd forgotten to take her key back from him? What was he doing at her house? Had he seen a light, maybe thought she'd returned home? Maybe imagined talking her into taking back the engagement ring? Into marrying him?

She shook herself. Hell, did the "why" even matter? He was dead. Like Dad. Like Nancy. Possibly like that poor man in Seattle. *Because of her.* Dear God, who would be next? Kenner? Luna? Some other innocent? Cade? Cody?

Fear collided with her shock, a shattering crash that snapped her lethargy. She gripped each side of the sink and forced herself to focus, her attention and her mind. Her eyes glittered back at her as dark and hard as green glass. With every last shred of her will, she had to prove her innocence.

But first, she had to get as far away as possible from her son and Cade. That, she knew, was something Cade would not allow.

She'd go without telling him.

Finding strength in this new resolve, she showered, dressed, applied her makeup carefully, changing the shape of her mouth and eyes, then donned the black wig. She'd swear the woman looking back at her in the mirror no longer resembled Joanna Edwards. She needed Cade's confirmation.

He and Cody were snuggled on the mussed sheets. Cade had put on undershorts, changed the baby's clothes, and was watching Cody devour his morning bottle. They were a painting waiting to be put to canvas, a touching vision that stole her breath, a memory she would take with her to recall and warm her heart on the lonely search ahead.

Cade's attention shifted toward her, his eyes widening, as though he'd been expecting a different sight to come through the bathroom door. She'd feared his sympathy, his pity, couldn't have stood either without falling apart again. She was glad she'd surprised him instead.

"What do you think?" she asked.

He nodded in approval. "If I didn't know who you were..."

"Good. Then I've accomplished what I set out to do. Why don't you take a shower? We have a lot to do before tonight. We can grab something at a fast-food place on the way," Joanna suggested, doubting she'd be able to keep anything down for a long time to come.

"Sure." He rose, pointing to Cody. "He's about ready to drop back to sleep anyway."

"I'll take over," she said.

Cade caught her hands and kissed them. He gathered fresh clothes and shaving gear and closed the bathroom door. Joanna went to the bed and sank down next to Cody. She touched his cheeks, his hands, his perfect little body, holding back tears now.

Oh, God, how did she say goodbye to her son when she'd only just found him? Her heart felt as though it were splitting down the middle. She heard water running in the bathroom sink. She had so little time. She lifted Cody, cradling him; the weight of his head, the warmth he created in the crook of her arm felt heavenly. He reached up to grab the wig, loosening the bottle from his mouth. "Mama."

Her soul seemed to shear off, to rip away from her. She wasn't sure she could do this. *But she had to.* She should be grateful for the few days she'd had with her son, but it was just too few.

She kissed him goodbye and laid him down in the travel bed.

In the bathroom, Cade was humming; his off-key enthusiasm for the song he was murdering endeared him to her all the more. How had she come to care so much for this man in such a brief span of time? She pressed her palm to the bathroom door, splaying her fingers as though she were caressing his flesh. He turned on the shower. She shook herself. She had to hurry. She snatched up a tablet and jotted him a note.

Knowing Cade was stubborn enough to come after her, she found the invitations to the art auction, tucked both into her purse, then dug into his pants pocket and came up with the keys to Lynne's SUV. Cade had stopped singing. Her pulse skipped. She opened the glass door. She glanced out from between the curtains. Someone was walking past. She pulled back, then reminded herself that her disguise was good. *Stay calm. Be smart.*

She stepped through the curtains.

An iron-strong hand grabbed her upper arm and yanked her back into the room.

Cade was naked, his face red with fury. He shook the note she'd written at her. ''Where the hell do you think you're going?''

Joanna gulped and struggled against his grip. ''Three people are dead because of me, possibly four. You or Cody could be next.''

''So you were just going to run out on us like Nan did? After last night, how could you?''

''It's because of last night that I have to. You have to let me go. Don't you see?''

''No. I don't.'' Anger flashed in his great eyes, but hurt shone in their depths. ''I thought we'd connected.''

She touched his freshly shaven cheek, aware that he was naked, and beautiful, and despite the hurt and anger, he trusted her enough not to be self-conscious about his nudity. But it was that very level of comfort that had her worried. She glanced sensuously at the most delicious parts of him, then lifted her gaze to his. ''Because of last night, because of *this,* we'll be distracted, our minds on things besides proving my innocence, because of last night, we've more to lose, and more ways to lose it.''

His stare narrowed. ''Nan's dead because she ran away. I could have protected her. She'd be alive now if she'd trusted me. You have to trust me, Joanna.''

"I do trust you." *Hell, I think I love you.* "I don't want anything to happen to you. Or to Cody. You have to let me go before someone discovers we're in Spokane together."

"They already know."

"What?"

"It's the only thing that makes sense." He released her and stalked to the bathroom, retrieving his clothes. She followed him. He stepped into his undershorts, then strode to the bed. He sat down and put on his socks.

He glanced up at her. "Someone started that fire last night just as we pulled up to your house. Otherwise, it would have been a five-alarm blaze by the time we discovered it. While we were in the house, he called the police, hoping you'd be caught there—with Bob's dead body."

She sank to the mattress beside him. "A-are you sure?"

"I'd stake every instinct I have as a cop on it." He pulled on his jeans, stood, zipped the fly, then sat again. "The blood on the kitchen floor hadn't started to coagulate yet."

"But how could someone know when we'd arrive at the house? We told no one."

"And I'd swear that no one followed us from the lake house."

"Then how? The only one who knew we were coming to Spokane was Luna."

"Yeah." He nodded, a curly lock of his dark, damp hair bouncing on his forehead.

Joanna stiffened, horrified at his unspoken suggestion. "You can't seriously think she's a suspect."

"I can't rule her out, either."

"Dear God, Cade, you've met her. Luna isn't physically capable of dragging a man of Bob's size from the kitchen to the studio. Especially not—" she hesitated "—not a dead body."

"Does she have help moving around those heavy metal sculptures and large paintings in her gallery?"

"Yes. Sometimes. But, Cade, we didn't tell Luna what time we'd be leaving for Spokane. We only talked about that in the SUV as we were driving out of Seattle. We were alone then."

They stared at one another a long moment digesting this. He tugged on a dark blue polo shirt. "Either someone bugged the SUV while we were in the Galleria, or they were following us when we left there, listening to us from a distance."

"Why didn't they just follow us to the lake house, then, and kill us there?"

"Because then someone would investigate and an investigation might lead the police to a link between you and the killer. Maybe even motivation. This way, they eliminate you and get off scot-free."

Fear slithered through her stomach. He reached for the remote to switch off the TV. But didn't manage it before they heard, "The hunt for Joanna Edwards has intensified."

Cade gripped her hand, kissing her temple, mumbling words of reassurance, trying to persuade her that he would keep her safe. But nothing he said convinced her that staying with Cody and him would keep *them* safe.

Everyone is looking for me, but the killer already knows where I am.

Chapter Fourteen

Over the next eight hours, Joanna mulled over her certainty that the killer knew her whereabouts, and she found fault in her reasoning. If he knew where she was, why wasn't she under arrest? Why risk having her show up at the art auction?

That was it, she realized, *that was it.*

The killer didn't know where she was because somehow she and Cade had eluded him the previous night. That meant whoever he—or she—was didn't realize they'd changed vehicles. In the dark, Lynne's SUV had probably looked like Cade's. The killer must have assumed it *was* Cade's, and hadn't bothered checking the license number.

That meant the killer would be waiting for them this evening. Would have set who knew what kind of trap. If only they knew for certain who that adversary was…. She bit her bottom lip, determined not to cave to the fear that would debilitate her.

She gazed across at Cade behind the wheel. Her heart skipped erotically, an odd sensation given the fear she hadn't quite squelched. But it was impossible to glance at him without remembering their lovemaking, without wanting to reexperience the pleasure he gave. Formal wear definitely suited this grandly beautiful man. The ebony and white of tuxedo and dress shirt made the blue of his eyes startling.

The only male at the auction who might snatch the most-handsome prize from him was Cody. She hadn't known they made tuxedos that small, or that her child could be more adorable than he already was.

For herself, she'd chosen a sleeveless, V-necked black sheath covered in bugle beads. She toyed with one of the beads. "Cade, what kind of design was on that button, could you tell?"

He scrunched his eyes a second, his expression thoughtful. "I'm not positive, but it looked like a fish of some kind, a dolphin maybe. Luna had something similar in that display case near her cash register."

Luna again. Joanna rolled her eyes. "What about Kendall Addison? I told you she said she had a protégé who designed jewelry. Maybe he has some sort of an affinity for dolphins. Maybe it's his signature design."

"We'll know soon enough," Cade said, driving through the gates of the Addison estate. Joanna exited the SUV and began walking up the driveway as Cade pulled ahead. She'd convinced him that she'd be safer alone, that anyone expecting her to be with him wouldn't automatically see through her disguise. He hadn't liked it, but he'd seen the wisdom in it.

She had her ticket in her small bag. Although none of her paintings would be on display tonight, it was unlikely whomever was collecting tickets would question whether or not she was one of the artists whose work was being auctioned.

She passed luxury vehicles of every size and shape, half expecting someone to jump out at her from behind one of them. Despite the warm air, she shivered and hugged herself. She watched Cade park at the front entrance, extract Cody from the back seat, then hand the keys and a tip to a valet.

She quickened her step up the short rise, an inexplicable urgency pressing her. The mansion occupied a knoll overlooking Lake Washington on Mercer Island. The architecture was one-of-a-kind, an oval, three-story building. Two-thirds of the ground floor was as open and huge as a ballroom in a palace, designed for large functions such as the art auction that was being held here this evening.

Slightly breathless, she arrived at the walkway as Cade and Cody reached the door. Just in case someone decided to give him a hard time about bringing a baby to this function, Cade was going to say he was security and Cody was his cover. He glanced back at her as if casually perusing the crowd. For the hundredth time in the last few hours, she was reminded how much she had to lose, of the risk they were taking just being here.

CADE STOOD inside the front door, getting the lay of the land, assuring himself that he could pick Joanna out in an instant—it was one of the benefits to being six foot four. Above the hum of a thousand or so voices, he caught the lilting sounds of a string quartet that, any other night, he might have enjoyed.

To his right, the room swept into a large backward capital C dominated by marble floors and glass walls with views to the sweeping gardens and the vast expanse of lake.

To his left, the room was short, a lowercase C. It held a wet bar. Guests who wanted something stronger than the champagne being circulated throughout by waiters clustered there in uneven queues.

Straight ahead, a curving chrome staircase hugged the solid wall that conjoined with the wall behind the wet bar. The stairs led up to the family levels to which a velvet rope denied access. A guard, dressed in black-tie and tails, was positioned to assure the barrier was not violated. His stern expression drew attention to the scar that severed his left eyebrow. He was one of the two who'd shown up at Cade's house the other day, the hired gun who'd shot Joanna's father. Had he killed Nan and Bob Massey? Run over that man near the Galleria?

Or was the killer they sought someone else?

Cade shifted Cody in his arms and stepped farther into the room. He needed to get upstairs, into the family's living quarters. He glanced once more toward the wet bar. Beyond it, behind the solid wall, Cade had made it his business to know that there was a private area with a service door for deliveries and an elevator for conveying stores to the second floor. Tonight the caterers would be using that elevator to supply guests with hors d'oeuvres and wine.

He figured it was the only way Joanna and he could get to the family levels, to Addison's private study. But the only access was at the far end of this building through all of the art displays. He merged with the milling crowd. From seven to nine, guests and bidders would be viewing the contributed artworks. The auction would begin in an hour or so, a sit-down affair. By then, Joanna and he had better be on the second floor.

He scanned again and spotted her moving toward the paintings that were hung from temporary partitions around the room. She was exquisite in that simple evening dress, a knee-length scrap of fabric that caressed her curves in ways he ached to replicate. There was no denying he'd been physically drawn to her from that first encounter, but the more time he spent with her, the more he learned about her, the more she fascinated him.

He'd never met another woman like her. Take the way she could change her appearance. Her talent in that area seemed endless. Tonight's makeup gave her emerald eyes a golden quality, a shade almost exactly that of Cody's eyes.

Not wanting to lose sight of her, Cade followed in her wake, lagging behind, guarding her from afar. No one seemed to be paying any attention to her, unlike Cody, whose presence needed explaining to a few of the attendees, and who garnered as many oohs and aahs as some of the artwork from others. He was shy in the huge crush of people, and kept pushing his head into Cade's neck.

He nuzzled his son, laughed and smiled at Cody. But his smile fell as he spied Luna Cassili chatting with Shane Addison. What the hell was going on? Of course, as a contributor Luna would know Addison. But, why hadn't she mentioned it the other day?

His mouth tightened. Holding Cody safely to him, he shifted through the press of bodies trying to get nearer, to hear what they were saying. But by the time he reached the spot where Addison seemed to be holding court, Luna was moving on and Addison was speaking to a prominent Seattle businessman and his wife.

Shane glanced toward him. Cade tensed. Pivoted. Pretended an interest in the displays. Every kind of art seemed to be represented, from paintings to metal sculptures to jewelry. *Jewelry*. Was the artist who'd designed the button represented here tonight? It was damn possible, Cade realized, wanting to talk to him or her. Still focused on making his way to the servants' entrance that would give him access into the elevator room, he scanned each exhibit he passed, cursory glances, his attention veering to Joanna every few minutes.

"Isn't this grand?" a woman asked to his right.

Cade lowered Cody to the crook of his arm and rotated toward the speaker. Kendall Addison. She hadn't spoken to him though, but to Luna and Mel Reagan. A vision in yellow and pink, Addison's wife brought to mind a summer sunset. Her dark eyes flashed with enthusiasm. She had one arm linked with Joanna's gallery-owner friend and was waving a champagne glass toward an exhibit of jewelry.

Cade peered over their heads and studied the items spread on a purple velvet cloth. A pendant caught his eye and wobbled his pulse.

Kendall enthused, "The artist is Shelldon Sharkey. A find."

"Is that pendant shaped like a shark?" Luna asked. She wore the shocking-red wig she'd had on yesterday and something that looked like a body-size aqua scarf. Gold beads and bobbles, sewn on the scarf without any discernible pattern, clanged and gleamed with her every movement.

"Shell uses the shark on his signature pieces," Kendall gushed. "I think he's a genius. You could do worse, Luna, featuring him at the Galleria."

"He likes shells, too." Mel Reagan was obviously unimpressed. Or was that jealousy in his eyes? He nodded at the jewelry Kendall wore: pink doodads that looked like shells attached to gold chains.

Cade fixed his gaze on the displayed pendant. The design looked the same to him as the one that had been on the bloodied button in Joanna's kitchen. Not a dolphin, he realized, but a shark.

"Cade, what are you doing here?"

"Ted?" Cade jerked around, as surprised to encounter his ex-brother-in-law in this setting as Ted Wheeler was to see him. "I might ask you the same thing."

"Abbot, Reed and Harrington are big supporters of Addison for governor." Abbot, Reed and Harrington was the law firm where Ted had his legal practice. Ted's eyes narrowed. "Do you realize the woman who was in your kitchen the other night is the one the police are looking for in connection with Nan's murder?"

"Lower your voice," Cade growled, gripping Ted's elbow and hauling him away from Shelldon Sharkey's jewelry exhibit and the three suspects who'd stopped talking to look at Ted with open mouths and curious gazes.

Ted shook Cade off. "You introduced her by some other name, but it was her all right. I'd know her anywhere. What was she doing there? What did she want? So help me, if you had anything to do with Nan's death—"

"I'm gonna forget you said that, Ted." Cade wanted to wring this man's neck. "I had no reason to kill Nan and you know it."

"Do I?" He glanced pointedly at Cody. Cody frowned at him. Ted sputtered, "Maybe you wanted to get rid of her so you could keep her kid all to yourself.''

''Be glad I have my son with me or I'd knock out what few brains you have left.''

''Okay, okay. No need to get hostile.'' He glanced nervously around, tugging on his vest.

Cade took the opportunity to steal a glance toward the Sharkey exhibit. All three of his suspects had scattered. Mel Reagan, he noted, was dangerously close to Joanna. Cade's mouth dried.

Ted tapped his arm. ''You're the last person I'd expect to see tonight.''

Cade made to move away from him. ''I'm a patron of the arts.''

''Yeah, right. Joanna Edwards is an artist.'' Distrust dripped from Ted. ''Your being here have *anything* to do with Nan?''

Cade stopped. ''Why would it?''

''Well, when I saw her last week, she told me about some trouble in Spokane last year.''

Cade scowled. ''You swore to me that you hadn't seen her.''

Ted blanched. He tried to get Cody to grip his fingers. Cody smacked his hand and reached for something attached to Ted's lapel.

Ted said, ''Nan made me promise not to tell you. She claimed you didn't do anything about this when she told you about it last year and she knew you wouldn't help her now. Then she took off again and I never saw her or heard from her after that.''

''If you're still lying to me...''

''I'm not.''

''You'd better not be. Now, what exactly did she tell you?'' Cade moved closer to him, pressing Ted against one of the glass windows, creating a private space for them and keeping his voice low, hoping Ted would do the same.

For once, Ted took the hint. "Seems a bomb was set off at the house of a woman she was hired to midwife. Her client was that Edwards dame, who, Nan said, accused Shane Addison of being behind the bombing."

Cade made a face.

"Look, pal," Ted continued, "my firm has a heavy investment in Addison. If he is somehow involved, I *have* to know."

"How do you plan to find out?" If he had a plan, Cade wanted to hear it. Needed to hear it. He'd be damned if Ted was going to mess up his and Joanna's plans.

"I don't know." Ted grew thoughtful, tugging on his vest again, then his tie as though it were strangling him. "I'll think of something. Maybe Addison knows where to find the Edwards woman. She sure wasn't at her house."

"She wasn't—?" Cade almost choked. "Her house in Spokane? You were in Spokane?"

"Yesterday." His eyes twitched. "Look, there's my boss. I have to pay my respects."

Ted raised a hand to someone, and pried Cody's fingers off the object attached to his lapel. That was when Cade realized what it was. A pin shaped like a button...with a shark embossed on it. "Where'd you get that?"

"What?"

"That pin?"

"Oh, this? Kendall Edwards sent them to the office. Excuse me." He skirted Cade and fled. Cade stared at his departing back, something clammy swimming in his gut. All this time he'd thought Ted was a buffoon. Had he underestimated the man at every level? Could Ted be more involved with the Addisons than he'd ever suspected?

Joanna. He freed his gaze and sped it around the room, seeking and finding her. He breathed easier. She was standing beneath a painting, a portrait. He lifted Cody to his chest and set a course for her, deciding to check on her, to tell her they were running out of time.

They had to get upstairs.

He slipped up beside her and whispered her name. She didn't move, just continued to stare at the painting. It was a mother and child. There was something familiar about the mother, and it took Cade a second to realize that she resembled Joanna. He found the signature and frowned. J.O.E.

The artist listed was J. Owen Eagle, the name Luna had said she'd use to submit Joanna's work. Was this one of the two paintings Luna had recently sold? He asked, "What is this?"

She didn't glance around. "It's one of the paintings that I did this past year. It should have burned up in the studio."

"How…?" He broke off, realizing she was wondering the same thing: Had the killer taken this last night and brought it here? Did this prove Luna was the killer? Considering Joanna's reaction every time he even suggested her friend was somehow involved in this, he held his tongue.

He studied the painting, his first chance to judge Joanna's work. He discounted the cityscape of Spokane, as he hadn't known it was hers when he'd viewed it. This had to be a self-portrait. Even with his untrained eye, he could tell it was good. Very good. Compelling. She'd titled it *Baby of Mine*. The woman in the painting was seated in a rocking chair, in a garden, her child cradled in her arms. She was gazing at the child with such love it tugged at his heart.

Instead of the colors of spring more appropriate to a garden setting, Joanna had chosen varying shades of blue and gray and white, managing to convey the sorrow that she had to have been feeling when she painted this. For only a woman who had loved and lost her child could have put that feeling on canvas. He said, "Don't worry. We'll find her."

"Her?"

"Your daughter, Maddy."

"Oh, yes." She seemed to choke on the words.

He wished he could touch her, take her hand, pull her to his side. Instead, he studied the baby in the portrait. Although months younger, this child looked oddly like Cody. It was spooky. Joanna hadn't known or even seen Cody before she'd created this painting. "Who modeled for the baby."

"I used my own baby pictures."

"Oh."

She whispered, "How did this painting get here?"

"I have a theory or two. Let's get upstairs and find out whether I'm right. Head to the far end of the room. When a waiter or waitress emerges from the private entrance, try and slip inside. We'll meet you there."

"Okay, but be careful, Cade. I spotted Detective O'Brien near the bar when I came in. No telling where he is now."

Chapter Fifteen

Keeping his eyes peeled for any sign of Detective O'Brien, Cade waited for Joanna to move ahead and begin weaving her way through the noisy horde. Unconsciously, he held Cody to his heart, protecting him from grabbing hands and admiring pinches. The baby plucked at Cade's tie, and Cade felt the tiny, strong fingers lock onto a corner. When Cody couldn't bring the tie to his mouth, he dipped his head to the tie.

Again, Cade marveled at how only a week ago he would have been appalled at the thought of a teething child slobbering on his formal attire. What a difference that child being his own made. He smirked and regarded his surroundings. No sign of O'Brien. The end of the room was in sight, but Joanna had stopped before a screen with a cluster of small paintings. Cade carried Cody toward the windows, needing to scope out the situation. She would wait until he gave her the go-ahead.

With his back to one of the structure beams that separated the windows, he scouted the layout and considered their options. The door was on the other side of the screen where Joanna stood. A waiter was coming through the door carrying a tray of filled champagne glasses. Joanna helped herself to one. She took a sip, peering covertly at Cade over the rim of her glass, a look of anticipation and something less detectible on her lovely face. Fear? Longing?

With an effort, he reined in the desire she roused in him, pulled his attention from everything he'd done, and would like to do again with and to this beautiful woman, and back to the task at hand. Next to the door, a man in a rumpled tuxedo—that might have been tossed into the lake and put on to dry—was mopping his bald head with a white hankie the size of a pillowcase.

Cade swore under his breath. Cody relinquished the tie and looked at Cade with a serious lowering of his eyebrows, his tiny fingers sliding into Cade's open mouth as though he were grabbing the cursewords out.

Chagrined, Cade extracted his son's fingers and glanced around. What he needed was to create a distraction. To his left he noticed an exhibit of metal sculptures lined up like dominoes. Perfect. Intentionally, he sidled to the display. Switched Cody into his other arm.

Cody, reacting as expected, was immediately intrigued and delighted with the shiny twisted objects that were precariously balanced on a strip of plywood. With a squeal of joy—and every baby's fearless certainty that whoever was holding on to them wouldn't drop them—he lunged sideways and tapped at the first of the sculptures.

"No," Cade scolded in a tender voice, moving away just as the first sculpture tipped into the second, then the second into the third, the third into the fourth. A loud clatter ensued. The exhibit toppled and crashed to the floor.

Appalled art patrons rushed forward. Cade retreated with Cody. The sweating guard joined the concerned guests, and Joanna ducked through the door into the elevator room. Cade, watching nothing now, except her delicious departing backside, made a beeline to follow.

A beefy hand landed on his shoulder, jerking him to a stop like a roped bull. "I keep running into you in the most interesting places."

Cade glanced over his shoulder to stare into the face of Detective O'Brien. The Tukwila policeman's smile was toothy and unfriendly. Cade swore to himself again, and mentally scrambled to come up with some way to get rid of him before the sweating man resumed his position at the elevator door.

"You don't return your calls," O'Brien said. "Why is that, Maconahey?"

Cade lifted an eyebrow at him and switched Cody to his other arm. "I don't know what you're talking about, Detective. Why don't you clear up my confusion?"

O'Brien's dark eyes narrowed. "Your answering machine. I've been leaving you messages since I saw you the other day at that hit-and-run down on Second Avenue."

As THE DOOR CLOSED silently behind her, Joanna felt fear trickle down her spine. She fought the feeling, but her breath came quick and fast. She sent her gaze in a rapid swirl through the long, narrow, well-lighted room. She was alone. She took another sip of champagne, for courage, wishing it were something stronger, like scotch. How did Cade stand the stress of undercover work? Sure, there was a kind of rush, but when she considered the consequences of being discovered and unmasked, her palms dampened and the hairs on her nape prickled.

She never felt anything close to this at her job. Rather, painting was calming, freeing, satisfying. Safe.

She was alone, she reminded herself. Perfectly safe. For the moment. She allowed herself to breathe easier.

Male voices on the other side of the door startled her. She tensed again. Neither voice belonged to Cade. What if one or both of the men should come in here ahead of him? Seeking a hiding place, she scanned the room. The elevator occupied the end wall, an oversize metal door the outer wall. Cade had told her this door was for deliveries. As though in testament to that, several cardboard boxes with food company logos were stacked haphazardly beside it.

That door, she decided, might provide a quick exit later. She hastened to it and unlocked the bolt.

Using the boxes as a screen, Joanna waited for Cade. She sipped the champagne. Two minutes passed, then four, then six. Where was he? She drained the glass. Still no Cade. What was taking so long? The liquor was not blunting her nerves as she'd hoped. Something—or someone—had detained Cade. But what? Who?

That Tukwila cop maybe? Addison? One of his henchmen?

An awful fear gripped her. Maybe she should go back into the exhibit room and make certain Cody and Cade were all right. She thought about Cade, about his towering strength, his powerful body, his intelligence, his savvy. His only vulnerability was Cody. But no one would pull something dangerous in this crowd on a man with a small baby.

Panic was scrambling her reasoning. She had to trust Cade. Trouble was, when thoughts of losing her son hit her, she trusted nothing. But if she left here and discovered Cade and Cody were fine, only detained, she might not be able to reenter this room. Damn. Patience was not proving her best virtue.

What should she do? She couldn't bear this waiting.

The whirring of the elevator motoring downward jarred her. She squeaked, and ducked behind the stack of boxes. A waiter emerged from the elevator, strode past and exited into the exhibit room, aided by the sweating guard, she saw, peeking from over the box tops.

Through the gaping door, she spotted Cody first, then Cade. Then O'Brien. Her mouth dried. The door shut, closing out her view, punctuating the fact that she was on her own, as alone as she had been three days ago before linking up with Cade and Cody, as alone as she'd intended to be earlier today when she'd tried to leave them in that motel in Spokane.

The idea of being alone felt right. It eliminated all risk to Cody.

Cade would understand that when she told him later.

She slipped quickly to the elevator. It opened within seconds. On the way up, she decided if she ran into anyone in the kitchen, she would act as though she were a houseguest. *God, please, let me get in and out of Addison's study with phone records I need before anyone comes investigating.*

The elevator slid open on a kitchen that was all shiny chrome surfaces, white-enamel starkness and catering mayhem. No one as much as glanced at her, intent as they were on loading trays with scraps of designer food and filling crystal long-stemmed glasses with champagne.

If she wasn't one of the help, she was not their concern.

Joanna breathed shallowly through her clenched teeth, scrutinizing the layout of the room, and finally locating the exit into the family quarters. She headed for it on the balls of her feet.

Through a set of swinging doors, she came out into a dining room, big, formal, with a view of the lake. The table was carved glass and brass, shaped to conform to the rounded curve of the window wall and would accommodate at least fifty diners. The chairs were high-backed and looked as though they would correct the lazy posture of anyone unlucky enough to sit in them.

No cozy breakfast nook, this. Joanna was glad her son would never partake of meals in this house. The room was as cold as Shane Addison's heart.

She skirted the table and a buffet hutch. As she neared the egress, the noise from the festivities on the floor below grew louder. She stepped forward with caution and peered through the doorway. The stairwell was ten feet from her. She couldn't see the guard stationed at the foot of the stairs and guessed he couldn't see her either.

She slipped out of the dining room, edged along the wall and into a vast living room with a view that seemed to serve as a huge mosaic. Here the furniture was overstuffed, cotton-chintz fabrics in varying hues of yellow. A golden room for a golden couple, it suggested. At the moment it was occupied only by the last rays of the setting sun.

Joanna turned her attention to the door farther along the wall. It was closed. Addison's study?

Hoping she was right, she crossed to it, leaned her head against the enameled surface of the door and listened. No sounds came from within. She gripped the doorknob. It opened easily. She stepped into a dark room, and groping, found a light switch. There was one long window covered with blinds that were closed, eclipsing the view and all natural light.

She eased the door closed. This was more than a study. It seemed to be a reception area for what might be a larger office beyond. She hadn't known Addison had his office at home, hadn't bothered to find out.

There were chairs against one wall, metal files behind a desk. Against another wall there was a copy machine. She moved to the desk. A leather-bound blotter abutted a laptop computer and a four-line telephone. The initials MVR were stamped into the lower right-hand corner of the leather. Mel Reagan?

She glanced at the door beyond the desk, certain now that it led to Shane Addison's office. The information she sought, however, could very well be here.

She yanked open a side desk drawer and peered into it. It seemed to contain only sticky-note pads and pens. Where would phone records be?

"What are you doing?" The angry male voice sliced through her, freezing her hand on the next drawer.

She recognized the voice. Mel Reagan. He had emerged from Addison's office. Joanna hadn't even heard the door open.

She heard him now, moving toward her. *She* couldn't move at all. She didn't look at him. "I—I need to use the phone and was looking for a phone book.''

"There are phones on the ground floor...with phone books.''

"I'm a houseguest of the Addisons—''

"No, you're not, Ms. Edwards.''

The pit of her stomach opened and all of her courage tumbled out. Joanna looked at Mel Reagan then. He was holding a gun on her. Somehow, she managed to say, "I knew you were behind this. Ever since my father contacted Shane about the baby, Shane has had you trying to kill us.''

"Your father contacted me, not Shane. I informed Addison about this mess only one month ago. He really doesn't remember you or believe that your child is his. Neither does Kendall. They want you to go away. Were willing to pay you to make you go away. But I knew you wouldn't. Your type never does. The minute you're offered money, you think you've tapped into a cash cow.''

Joanna's eyebrows arched upward. This man had taken it upon himself to kill people rather than pay for her silence. Her father, Nancy Wheeler, Bob, and maybe even some innocent guy she'd never even seen. She balled her hands at her sides, holding back the urge to throw herself at Reagan and hammer him to the ground with her fists.

"Well, that isn't happening this time,'' he continued. "Addison is going to be governor soon and one day president. I intend to be by his side for the whole ride. He's not going to be brought down by a bimbo like you.''

"I'm not trying to bring him down. All I ever

wanted was to be left alone. I'm not a threat to you. Or to Addison. I never was.''

His expression faltered, then hardened. "Yeah, right. Believe me, I've grown expert at dealing with the likes of you.''

Joanna swallowed at the implication. How many other of Addison's former lovers were alive to tell about it? None from the sound of it. This man was pure evil. She took a step back from him.

"Oh no you don't.'' He gestured toward the bigger office behind him. "Get in there.''

She looked from the barrel of the gun, an expanse as long as her lifetime and Cody's, to the cold dark eyes of the man holding her life in his hands. He meant business, of that she was certain. Only a fool with nothing to lose would defy him. She had everything to lose. But she'd be damned if she wanted him to see how scared she was. Defiantly, she lifted her chin. "Why should I go in there with you?''

"Because we're going to call the police and have you arrested.''

We?

Chapter Sixteen

Joanna stumbled on boneless legs into Shane Addison's office, influenced by the gun barrel being poked against her spine. There was someone sitting in the high-backed leather chair behind the massive brass-and-glass desk. Someone she couldn't see. Shane Addison? Kendall? The man who'd killed her father? The guy with the sweat-gland problem?

Or someone she didn't even suspect?

Fear threatened to panic her. She had to buy time. Had to get away. Prayed Cade would arrive and rescue her. Thought of Cody and prayed Cade wouldn't show up at all.

She was on her own. She'd chosen to do this without help. She had to save herself.

"Look," she said. "If you have me arrested, I'll tell the whole world what a louse Shane Addison is. I'll sell my story to the *Weekly Tattler*. It will end that family-value platform he's been running on. Not only won't he make it to the governor's mansion, but you can kiss goodbye your dreams of sleeping in the White House."

A magenta hue colored Reagan's face like a mask, hiding his intentions, but not his fury. His dynamic personality sizzled the air between them, giving off a scary heat. He raised his voice speaking to the person in the chair. ''I told you we should have had her killed, too.''

Should have had her killed. So, neither of these two had dirtied their own hands. They'd had their thugs do the actual killing. Again rage swept through her, stronger than any of the other emotions that assailed her. She dug her nails into her palms until the pain was intense, barely holding her temper in check. These two people had destroyed her life, murdered people she loved, family members, friends. Had stripped her of her son, her father, her work. It was all she could do not to vent her fury on them.

Her gaze steadied on the gun in Mel Reagan's hand. She had to stay calm. To think this out. Not react to her ire.

''Having her arrested might solve other problems,'' Mel said, speaking to the person in the chair, the one Joanna still could not see. ''But it won't guarantee her silence.''

Too incensed to be terrified, Joanna swore silently, mentally kicking herself for not thinking to bring a pocket tape recorder. For here was the proof she needed: an actual and unexpected confession.

''She *is* going to be silenced, darling.'' The voice coming from the person in the high-backed desk chair was so familiar, it poleaxed Joanna. Her knees quaked. She stumbled to a low-slung leather chair that faced the desk and caught it for support. Her gaze fixed on the other chair, the high-backed one behind the desk where the Judas sat.

The chair slowly wheeled in her direction. The woman rose amid a clang of beads and flashes of light as the dying sun caught and glinted off the bubbles covering her Indian sari.

Joanna gaped at her best friend. "Luna?"

Before Luna could answer, Mel said, "I hope to hell you've got a contingency plan, 'cause we're gonna have to get her out of here without anyone wondering what we're doing."

"We're not going to get her out of here," Luna said.

"What? We have to." Mel's voice raised. "If she dies here there will be an investigation and we're back to square one trying to protect Addison."

"I'm not trying to protect him." Luna grinned maliciously, as though Mel was too stupid to understand what was really going on here. "That was always *your* motivation, not mine. We aren't taking Joanna anywhere. This is where I want her, where I've always meant her to be. The only place that I can exact revenge on both her and Shane."

"R-revenge?" Joanna sputtered. All she'd been put through this past year was a plot for revenge? Revenge for what? What had *she* ever done to Luna? Except be her friend? "What are you talking about?"

Luna narrowed her eyes and glared at Joanna. "Shane was mine. He was *always* mine."

Always? There was a timelessness in the way Luna had said that word. Always, as in forever, long ago. Joanna's mouth dropped open as she realized what Luna was telling her. "Shane fathered the baby you had when you were thirteen?"

She nodded. "He was seventeen at the time. My father swore he'd kill the guy who got me pregnant...and he would have. So I wouldn't tell him. We kept seeing each other after that, but we were careful.

He only married Kendall because of her money. His father made him. But it was me he loved.''

Joanna could not believe this. ''Why didn't you ever tell me?''

''Because you didn't need to know. No one did. It was *our* secret. He promised me he'd get a divorce when I was old enough to marry him.''

''But—?''

''Yeah, but! Year after year, I kept believing his lies. Every time I protested too much, he would give me something to keep me quiet. Like my gallery. For a while his guilt over my alopecia was enough to keep him under my thumb. My mistake was thinking a man who cheated on his wife could be trusted not to cheat on me.

''Especially not with my best friend.'' Her mouth bent downward.

''But he saw your picture in my apartment, that one you sent after getting settled in Paris. He asked me all kinds of questions about you. I was so naive, I never even suspected what he was up to. He must have taken your address off the envelope the photo came in, then he set up a business trip to Paris. He looked you up and made it seem an accidental encounter. Shane doesn't do anything by accident.''

Joanna felt as though a train had slammed into her headlong. The whole thing had been calculated, planned; he'd stalked her like an obsessed fan, a rapist, a seducer. She shuddered.

''What are you saying?'' Mel started toward Luna, shaking his head, disbelief and revulsion vying for control of his expression. ''You and Addison?''

''You don't really think I came after you for your good looks, now, do you, Mel?'' Luna laughed, a cruel cackle that Joanna had never guessed she could produce. "I needed you and your little band of merry baddoers."

His nostrils flared. "Why, you little bit—"

Luna stepped toward him, raising her arm as she moved, bringing a gun with a silencer from between the folds of her dress. She shot Mel Reagan in the chest. He dropped to the floor with a surprised look on his face. A scarlet circle appeared on his white shirtfront, quickly growing larger and larger.

As he lay dying, Luna glared down at him. "My plan all along was to kill Joanna in such a way that she would be linked with Shane. Doing it here will work just fine. She'll be accused of shooting you, Mel, darling, and you'll be accused of shooting her."

"But, why?" Joanna asked. "We were friends. Best friends."

"You betrayed me."

"Not intentionally. I didn't know about you and Shane. He lied to me the way he lied to you. I didn't even know his real name."

"He is a liar."

Joanna glanced at Mel Reagan, then back at Luna. "Don't do this, Luna. Let me call someone for Mel. Let me help you."

"Oh, get over yourself. The only thing I want from you are your paintings."

"But they were all burned in the fire in my studio."

"Fool." Luna laughed coldly, and Joanna blanched, belatedly recalling *Baby of Mine* displayed in the exhibit downstairs.

"That's right." Luna arched her drawn-on eyebrows. "I removed them before that fire was ever set. The day you left to go to Maconahey's house. That buffoon, Bob, even as angry as he was at you, helped me load them into my van.''

''Is that why you killed Bob?''

''Didn't you hear Mel? *I* killed no one. *He* ordered those killings.''

''That's not true, is it? You left that shark button in the blood in order to lead the police to Shane or Kendall. You were the only one who would have done that.''

Luna smirked, but didn't deny it. ''Aren't you the least bit interested in *where* your other paintings are?''

''I suppose they're stored in your warehouse.''

She squared her shoulders. ''Yes. And once you're dead, they're legally mine. Remember that sweet little clause in your will, giving them all to me? When you told me about that, I thought you were a pompous ass. Your paintings weren't worth the canvas they're painted on to the art world.''

Luna moved toward Mel's prone body. ''Then I discovered Shane's betrayal with you. I realized if there was a big enough scandal, one that culminated in your death, those paintings would have notoriety. They would sell for outrageous prices, making me a very rich woman.''

Joanna stepped toward the door. ''If all you wanted was money—''

''Money isn't all I want. Weren't you listening? I want you dead.'' Luna squatted beside Mel, laid down the gun with the silencer on the carpet. Mel still clutched his gun. Luna clasped the hand with the gun, aimed the barrel at Joanna and pulled the trigger. The recoil jerked the pistol and Luna's arm.

Joanna lunged sideways. The booming blast resounded in her ears. Out of the corner of her eye she saw the door to the office open. Saw a man. Saw him pitch backward as the bullet struck him. She hadn't seen who it was. Her attention was riveted to Luna.

The only detail she noted was that the man wore the same gleaming style of black shoe that Cade had been wearing.

Dread spasmed her throat. Luna was bringing Mel's arm around again. Aligning the sights with Joanna's chest again. Readying to pull the trigger again.

Joanna scrambled to her feet, bent at the waist and charged at Luna like a lioness at her prey, head-butting her right in the breadbasket. The smaller woman *whoofed* out air. The gun fired. The explosive report reverberated in Joanna's ears. Luna sailed toward the wall of windows. She landed with a cry, her spine thumping a support beam.

Joanna staggered up. She wasn't shot. Wasn't bleeding. Light-headed, she wobbled to the desk, her legs feeling bruised, her gait unsteady. She gathered the gun with the silencer. The other was still in Mel's hand. She turned, breathless, toward the man lying in the doorway. She couldn't see his upper body. Had no idea who he was or how badly he was hurt. Shock fell over her like a numbing quilt. "Cade?"

Her legs gave out then and she sank hard to the floor, her body quivering.

Voices and footsteps clambered toward the offices. The first person into the room was Detective O'Brien, his gun in hand. "Drop the gun!" he told her.

"She's Joanna Edwards," Luna shouted, still trying to pull off this awful revenge she'd plotted. *It would be her word against mine, Joanna realized. And who is going to believe me?* The only witness was dead.

The only other possible witness was bleeding in the doorway. Maybe, he was also dead.

O'Brien had assumed a stance that showed he was prepared to use his weapon. "Put the gun down, Ms. Edwards. You're under arrest."

Chapter Seventeen

Cade's heart thudded so hard it hurt. Joanna's name banged through his head, a mantra of fear as loud as the gunshots he'd heard from overhead. She had touched him in a place he thought had died years ago—as far back as childhood, when he'd given up hope of being adopted, of ever really belonging to anyone, to any family. He couldn't lose her. Not without a chance to explore the possibilities.

Cody couldn't lose her. Not if she was half the woman Cade knew she was. And her daughter...they all needed her. Please God, let her be okay.

He ran with Cody clutched to his chest. He reached the upper landing, arriving on O'Brien's heels. But at the entrance to the offices, he pulled back. As much as he wanted to rush in there and make certain that Joanna was well, safe, among the living and un-wounded, he hung back, restricted by Cody, unwilling to put his son at risk without knowing for certain what danger lay in that room.

From his vantage point, he watched O'Brien charge through a small office, stop, bend, examine a man on the floor of a second doorway. Cade's pulse skipped faster. He recognized that red hair. Ted. O'Brien moved past Ted and into the other room. He had his gun drawn and was taking on an attack stance that Cade knew all too well. Where was Joanna?

Cade heard a woman shout, ''She's Joanna Edwards.''

Next, O'Brien told someone to ''Drop the gun.''

Cade's gaze swept Ted. Blood stained his jacket near his waist and was pooling on the floor beneath him. Cade couldn't see the wound from where he stood, could not judge its severity. He moved toward him, then pulled back, torn between rushing in and waiting until O'Brien assured him it was safe.

O'Brien shouted, ''Maconahey, call for backup. Get an ambulance and the M.E.''

Cade hurried into the first office, grabbed a phone and dialed 911. When he'd made certain all the necessary professionals and emergency equipment were on their way, he set Cody into a corner away from the door and blocked him there with an overturned chair. He went to check on Ted, found that a bullet had gone clean through the love handle on his right side. It was bleeding profusely, but the bullet had likely hit no vital organs.

He fished his hankie from his pocket and stuffed it against the wound, took Ted's hand and pressed it to the hankie. Ted's eyes squinted open. He was pale. Cade assured him, ''The ambulance is on its way.''

Cade realized O'Brien was reading someone the Miranda. He glanced past O'Brien and spied Joanna. She was plunked on the floor, not unlike the first time he'd come up on her in his house, showing too much leg, those long lovely legs. She looked stunned. The black wig sat askew on her head, wisps of taffy-colored hair hanging down. Her makeup was smudged, her eyes wide with shock, horror. She was alive. Beautifully, wonderfully alive…and unharmed as far as he could tell.

But still in danger. Damn O'Brien and his determination to bring her in. Cade wanted to stop him, but what proof did he have that O'Brien would listen to?

His heart sank. He glanced at Cody, who was wriggling back and forth behind the chair, delighted to be free after the restriction of being held all evening. Near Cade's feet, Ted groaned, trying to say something. Cade couldn't hear him. He squatted. "What?"

Ted moaned. "Tell him the other one."

"The other what?" Cade scowled.

"The other one. Joanna didn't shoot anybody. That redhead did."

Luna? He knew it, but learning that he was right in his assumptions at this point gave Cade no satisfaction. "O'Brien, don't let the other one near a weapon. Read her rights to her, too."

"Why?" O'Brien's head shifted in Luna's direction.

"Just do it," Cade said in his sternest voice. "Our witness here says she's the one who shot him."

"No. He's dead," Luna screamed and raced for Mel's gun one more time. O'Brien shouted for her to stay where she was. She froze. Her face suddenly crumpling, all the painted-on prettiness slipping like the facade it was.

O'Brien took the gun from Joanna's grasp, handed it to Cade, then went to handcuff Luna. "Will our witness testify to that in court?"

"Yes. He's an attorney with Abbot, Reed and Harrington. He's also Nancy Wheeler's brother, in case you didn't notice."

O'Brien began reading Luna her rights.

Cade went to Joanna, taking her cold hand in his. He reached to pull her into his arms, ached to hold her near, to reassure himself that she was truly as unharmed as she appeared to be.

She warned him off. Gesturing toward the Tukwila police officer, she mouthed, "Don't."

Cade realized she was right. If he swept Joanna into his arms, O'Brien would realize he'd known who she was all along. She was trying to save his career. He pressed his lips in a tight line and nodded.

He helped her up. She swayed and, God, how he wanted to hold her. Instead, he steadied her by the elbow. She whispered, "Where's Cody?"

Cade's affection for her swelled. Her concern for him and his son were the first things on her mind. She was amazing. "He's in the other room."

"Is the man in the doorway okay?"

"It's Ted. He'll back up whatever story you have to tell. He was, I'd bet, eavesdropping. His testimony will hold weight." He squeezed her elbow. "You'll have to go to the station, give a statement, but I doubt charges will be brought against you."

Cade was right. Charges were brought against Luna Cassili. Warrants were issued for Juarez Romero, the man with the scar through his eyebrow, and Gerry Geeter, the sweating man.

Chapter Eighteen

It was after midnight before the police were satisfied that Joanna had had nothing to do with Nancy Wheeler's or Bob Massey's deaths. It was finally over. All the terror and horror. All the running scared. She was battle-scarred and had lost some of the most important people in her life, but her paintings had survived and, miraculously, she had found her son.

The problem was, she didn't know how to claim him. What could she say to Cade? How could she prove what she knew to be the truth?

All the way to the lake house to return Lynne's SUV, she had tried to figure out how she would broach the subject. But they were here now and she still had no idea. Neither Cade nor she had been in a talkative mood since leaving the police station. She felt overwhelmed, was still processing the things that had occurred, the things she'd learned.

The fact that the person she'd thought was her best friend, the one she'd shared her most personal and private feelings and dreams with since she was thirteen, was the biggest lie of all. She realized now that the facade Luna presented the world hid a hurt and jealous woman behind lavish wigs and flamboyant clothes. But what of the real woman? Had Luna ever shown her true self to Joanna? And if so, how would Joanna know when those times had been? Which of her memories were lies? Which were not?

The pain of it weighed heavy on her heart, a heart that had had too much to bear in a short time. She'd been too angry to grieve for her father. Too terrified to grieve for Nancy. Too shocked to grieve for Bob. Too busy surviving and hunting for their killers. The grief had not yet found her, but she sensed it coming, sensed it would soon break through the numbing aftermath of all she'd endured.

She was certain Cade was feeling something similar. After all, he'd loved Nancy enough to conceive a child with her. Even if he was mistaken about that. Cody was now fast asleep. He'd fallen asleep in Cade's arms hours ago. Joanna couldn't bear the thought of ripping this child from him, of breaking this kind and generous man's heart.

The only other choice was to walk away from Cody, and that was no choice.

Cade parked the SUV and got out. She exited too, retrieving Cody from the back seat, hugging him to her, feeling such love and contentment with this child in her arms that tears filled her eyes.

Cade was at the rear of the SUV, opening the hatch. He said, "I have a surprise for you."

She had a surprise for him, too, Joanna thought, *an unpleasant one, one that would be better presented here, on neutral ground. For she couldn't bear returning to his house in Auburn.* She went into the lake house, leaving the door open for Cade, carrying Cody to the rocking chair that was positioned near the potted plants. She sat down and gently rocked him. His face was so precious, his thick lashes dark against the pink roundness of his cheeks. His head was heavy on her arm, a welcome weight that she had missed for seven long months, and wanted never to miss again.

Cade came in, interrupting her thoughts, shattering the peace of the moment, bringing nearer the hour that she would break his heart. Instead of the baby bed she'd expected him to bring in, he was holding a painting. "I retrieved this from the exhibit."

Baby of Mine.

"How?" Joanna couldn't believe it. "Why?"

"How was the easy part." He didn't elaborate, just grinned at her, his whiskered jaw in need of shaving. "I was afraid one of the Addisons might realize it was your work and destroy it, or render it unsalable."

She glanced at the painting and then at Cody. "It's not for sale."

Cade was struck by how much she and Cody looked in that moment like a mirror reflection of the portrait. The muscles of his throat strained, and in the pit of his stomach he felt an uneasy pang, an old sensation, one of loss and disappointment, that he'd felt as a kid every time something he wanted was about to be snatched from him. "Too personal?"

"Yes." She looked at the baby and then at Cade. There was a sadness in her eyes that filled him with an inexplicable foreboding.

Ignoring his queasy gut, denying all the signs that something vile was about to befall him, he propped the painting against the sofa and went to her, lifting her hand to his lips, kissing it. "Don't worry. We'll find your daughter. There has to be something that will lead us to her. I won't give up until you're holding her in your arms...like in your painting."

"There's something I need to tell you, Cade." Her voice was too kind, too compassionate. "I'm not sure how to say this, how to convince you."

"How to convince me?" He was struck again by the way her eyes reminded him of Cody, how the baby in the portrait reminded him of Cody. Why was that? His instincts warned him not to ask, not to examine it too closely.

But as his gaze met hers he knew the truth, it was there in her eyes, on her face, in the way she held his son, *her son?* The realization was a death blow to his heart. No. No. No. It couldn't be true. It mustn't be true. But it was the only thing that explained Nan's being on the run for seven months, the only thing that explained why she hadn't come to him straight away after Cody's birth. He couldn't breathe.

"Nan wasn't pregnant. She didn't have a baby." Joanna's confirming words were like nails plunging into his brain. "Cody is *my* son."

Cade felt as though she'd run him through with a sword and left his lifeblood pouring out. He sank back on his haunches. His gaze devoured his son. *His son. His son. Not his son.* "No. No. You had a baby girl."

"They lied to me about that."

"It's not true. You're the one who's lying." But was she? He closed his eyes against the pain, a memory flashing through his mind: Joanna passing out cold in his bedroom when he'd shown her the photograph of Nan. She'd gone white with shock, been so startled. She'd reached out to Cody just before she'd fainted. No. No. He lifted his eyes to her now. "Give me my son."

"He's my son," she whispered. "Mine."

Cade's arms were outstretched, reaching for Cody.

Joanna relinquished her sleeping son. Cade hugged the baby to him, kissing his hair, his cheeks, his temples, an odd sheen in his eyes, pain etched in every line of his face.

A similar pain tore at her heart. *She had done this to him. She and Nancy and her father and Luna. They shared the responsibility for devastating this man, for ruining his life, but only she was left to deal with it, with him.*

She reached out to touch his arm. "I'm so sorry."

He pulled away, scowling at her. More hurt than anger on his face. "You lied to me. Just like Nan. Why didn't you tell me right away?"

His pain reached into her, tore at her heart. If she could stop his hurting she would. But she couldn't. She had no relief for him and it was killing them both. At least he was no longer denying the truth. "I couldn't tell you. I had to keep Cody safe."

Red swept up his neck. "How did lying to me keep him safe?"

Joanna blinked with a sudden understanding of that which had been obscured. She felt as though a cloud had parted in her mind, bringing revelation, showing her the reason for all the deception. Dear God, she'd done to Cade what her father had done to her. She hated Lonnie for the lies. Just as Cade now hated her. Only in this moment did she realize and accept that her father hurt her in order to protect Cody and her. Out of love and concern, not malice. "That was why Nancy lied to you. Like my father, she knew it was the only way to deter the person intent on killing me and my baby."

"And that's supposed to make it all right that everyone lied to me about the most important thing in my life?''

"Please, Cade. As long as you thought Cody was yours, really believed it—as I really believed my baby was dead—you acted on that belief and no one suspected his real identity. His real parentage. You saved his life."

"Thank you for disregarding my feelings in all of this." He rocked back and forth on his haunches. His whole body wrapped around Cody. "For not trusting me."

For ripping his heart out of his chest, she thought. "I couldn't let my feelings for you override my son's safety. He had to be my first priority. He was your first priority, too."

Cade pressed his lips together, resting his chin on Cody's head. That lonely glint was back in his eyes. But it seemed vast now, a gulf that was unfathomable, bottomless. She touched his hand, his great large hand that could be so tender with a woman, so gentle with a child. He pulled back again, and she knew she couldn't reach him, that he needed time alone to say goodbye to Cody. She rose and left them.

In the morning, Cade was gone. A rental car in his name was parked next to the house. Joanna took her son and went home to Spokane.

OVER THE NEXT eight weeks, the art auction scandal—as the papers were calling it—raged on. Luna gave an exclusive to a reporter at the *Seattle Times* and the stories were picked up on the APO wire service and carried in the *Spokane Daily*. Mel Reagan's participation eventually made it into the mix.

The Addisons denied knowing anything about the

crimes perpetrated against Ms. Edwards and her family. But Shane withdrew his bid for governor, sold the house on Lake Washington and moved his family to the East Coast.

Joanna ignored most of it. She'd lived it for too long and was glad now not to have to think about it. What she couldn't stop thinking about was Cade.

She'd be holding Cody and Cade's face would fill her mind. She'd be laughing at something Cody had done and would absently turn to tell Cade about it. But he was there only in her memories. In bed at night, she would dream of him, imagine the three of them in a grocery store selecting items for dinner, doing the everyday chores any real family would do together, imagine she and Cade alone, making love, feel his kisses sweeping her senses, his hands warm and large on her body.

Several times a day, she picked up the phone and started dialing his number, only to stop before it began to ring. He'd walked away without speaking to her. Without so much as saying goodbye. Cody was the one he loved, the one he'd held that last night.

Not her.

She'd finally found a man she could trust, and *he* didn't trust her.

She glanced around the living room of this house she'd shared with her father since childhood. The paintings she'd retrieved from the warehouse in Seattle were stacked about the walls, but it wasn't the clutter that made her feel that this was no longer home. It was empty of the warmth that a home should have, that she'd felt with Cade. Every corner reminded her of all that she'd lost, of all the pain and misery of the year, the last months.

Maybe she should sell the place. Leave the ghosts of her past and start fresh in a new house, with a new studio. Someplace that would be hers and Cody's. The more she considered this, the more she liked the idea.

She could afford it now, too. Luna had been right about one thing: the scandal roused a great deal of interest in her art. She'd made enough off the sale of three of the paintings to have the studio rebuilt. That, added to the profit Luna had made on the first two watercolors and the sale of this house, would more than cover her wishes.

The contractor was arriving this morning to go over the contract for the new studio. She'd have to explain that she'd changed her mind. She'd contact him again when she'd relocated.

She busied herself feeding Cody, calling a Realtor and setting up an appointment to list the house and look at others. She cleaned Cody off and took him in the living room to play a few minutes before she put him down for his morning nap.

Cody was growing by leaps and bounds. He responded to "patty-cake" by clapping his hands. He puckered his lips and made a smacking noise in response to "kisses." He had passed the pulling-himself-up-on-everything stage and would, for a few seconds, stand on his own with his tiny toes curled into the carpet for support. She expected he'd be walking soon.

He slapped his palms on the coffee table, quickly traversing from one end to the other, giggling. His laugh was infectious. His eyes were getting greener by the day and would soon, she suspected, be the same color as her own. She was glad he looked more like her than Addison. She dreaded the day she'd have to tell him about his birth father.

She'd rather tell him about the man who should have been his father, a giant of a man with a tender touch and a sweet soul. Tears burned her eyes and she stared at the phone, fighting the urge to call him.

Hell, didn't he miss Cody? Of course he did. Then why didn't he call and find out how he was?

Bolstered by her peeved mood, she reached for the phone and dialed. His answering machine picked up. "Leave a message at the beep." Curt, to the point, and yet, the sound of his voice sent warm shivers through her, stirred erotic memories, such delicious memories.

The machine beeped. She said nothing. Then hung up, feeling foolish, knowing his caller ID would record her number. Well, okay. The ball was in his court. If he didn't return the call, then that was the end of it. She'd reached out to him. He would have to reach out to her now or forget it.

Her doorbell rang. The contractor. She hurried to the door, peered through the peephole and saw a familiar face. Not the man she was expecting, but definitely someone who could build a studio. She frowned and eased open the door. "Mr. Fast?"

"Yep." It *was* Dale Fast, the Auburn contractor whom Cade had hired to turn his guest room into a nursery. "I understand you want to build a studio."

"Well, yes, but who told you that?"

"I did." Cade stepped into her line of vision. Joanna's heart skipped. He held an armload of roses, pink ones, red ones and yellow ones. He must have bought out a greenhouse. He offered them to her. "From my garden."

She checked a smile. She couldn't be bought this easily. God, he looked gorgeous, big and lean and all male in his tight blue jeans and navy polo shirt. "You didn't call."

"Or write." He smirked, sheepish, uncomfortable. "When I woke up that morning, I went straight to the station and got myself assigned to a new undercover case. I didn't want to think about my life. Didn't want to feel anything or figure anything out. I was mad at the world and I wanted to stay mad."

"Er, Mr. Maconahey, why don't I go take a look at that studio while you and Ms. Edwards hash out whatever it is?" Dale Fast didn't wait for an answer. He turned off the porch and started around the house.

"Stay on the stepping stones," Cade warned.

"It's okay," Joanna said. "I've had Dad's booby traps removed."

"Are you going to invite me in?"

She moved aside and he entered. Cody's face lit up when he saw Cade. He stayed standing at the coffee table, grinning and jabbering, then slapping the tabletop. Cade's face mirrored her son's. She took the roses into the kitchen, giving her two favorite males a few minutes to get reacquainted. She set the flowers in the sink. It touched her that he'd brought her roses he'd grown with his own hands. He must have stripped the bushes clean.

The aroma was strong and sweet and followed her back into the living room. Cade was sitting on the floor, holding her son. He glanced up as she came in. "He's getting big. His hair is longer."

"Yes."

Cade set Cody on the floor and stood. Cody crawled to the coffee table again and pulled himself up.

"So, you've been on a case." She shoved her hair back from her face on one side, self-conscious, fiercely glad to see him, at the same time terrified.

"I had plenty of time to think. To consider what I want and need."

"Yeah, me too."

He came to her, lifted his hand to touch her, but didn't. "I need to know if I'm the only one who thought we were great together."

"We were wonderful together." He was standing so near she ached to step into his arms. He'd made her feel things she'd never thought possible, dream dreams she'd never imagined could be hers. In turn, she'd ripped his heart out and left him in tatters. Now he was here claiming he'd figured it all out. It couldn't be that simple. In eight weeks of going over and over it, she had not come up with a solution.

"I don't think it will ever work, Cade. I'd always be wondering if you wanted me for myself, or if you wanted me because I have your 'son.'"

"If you remember that night at the Red Lion the way *I* remember it, then you know it's *you* I want. You're haunting my dreams, lady. Asleep and awake. Cody is just the cherry on top. I want the whole sundae."

"Won't you always wonder if you could trust me? If I really loved you or if I'd married you because I felt guilty for what I'd done to you?"

"You didn't do anything to me that I wouldn't have done to you. You were right. I would have gone to whatever lengths it took to keep this little guy safe, no matter the cost. I don't blame you for that. You did what you had to do. What any mother would do. Any father. Any parent."

"What happened to Cade the loner...who doesn't do partners?"

He glanced at his feet, then at her a bit sheepishly. He plowed a hand through his sienna hair, loosening a lock that fell across his forehead. His cerulean eyes crinkled at the corners, and a smile spread over his face making him look younger, boyish, heart-touchingly dear. "I can't stand my own company these days. I keep turning to speak to you, to share things with you...and you're not there. I need you there."

She understood *that* feeling. But there were things she didn't understand. "Why did you bring Dale Fast here?"

"Presumption on my part. I wanted him to see what kind of studio he'd have to build you if you accepted my marriage proposal and agreed to move to Auburn."

Joanna's pulse gave a hopeful skip. "Marriage proposal? Is that what this is?"

"I know it probably seems quick to you, but I've waited my whole life for a family. With Cody and you, I've finally got a shot at one. What do you say?"

He touched her then, skimmed his knuckles from her temple to her jaw, tugged her chin close and kissed her, a grazing brush of his mouth on hers. "I love you, Joanna. Please, give us a chance."

Joanna didn't have to think twice; she'd spent eight miserable weeks thinking. Sometimes a woman had to act. "And I love you, Cade Maconahey." She moved into his open arms for another kiss, a deeper kiss.

Cody said, "Dadadadadadadadadada."

Laughing, Cade and Joanna moved apart and glanced at their son, just in time to see Cody take his first step.

HARLEQUIN®

INTRIGUE

opens the case files on:

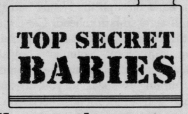

TOP SECRET BABIES

Unwrap the mystery!

January 2001
#597 THE BODYGUARD'S BABY
Debra Webb

February 2001
#601 SAVING HIS SON
Rita Herron

March 2001
#605 THE HUNT FOR HAWKE'S DAUGHTER
Jean Barrett

April 2001
#609 UNDERCOVER BABY
Adrianne Lee

May 2001
#613 CONCEPTION COVER-UP
Karen Lawton Barrett

Follow the clues to your favorite retail outlet.

HARLEQUIN®

Makes any time special ™

Meet 50 loving dads in

Take 4 FREE BOOKS,
Plus get a FREE GIFT!

bies & Bachelors USA is a heartwarming new collection of reissued
vels featuring 50 sexy heroes from every state who experience the
s and downs of fatherhood and find time for love all the same. All
the books, hand-picked by our editors, are outstanding romances
some of the world's bestselling authors, including Stella Bagwell,
stine Rolofson, Judith Arnold and Marie Ferrarella!

Don't delay, order today! Call customer service at
1-800-873-8635.
Or
Clip this page and mail it to The Reader Service:

In U.S.A.
P.O. Box 9049
Buffalo, NY
14269-9049

In CANADA
P.O. Box 616
Fort Erie, Ontario
L2A 5X3

! Please send me four FREE BOOKS and FREE GIFT along with the next four
els on a 14-day free home preview. If I like the books and decide to keep them, I'll
just $15.96* U.S. or $18.00* CAN., and there's no charge for shipping and
dling. Otherwise, I'll keep the 4 FREE BOOKS and FREE GIFT and return the rest.
decide to continue, I'll receive six books each month—two of which are always
—until I've received the entire collection. In other words, if I collect all 50 volumes,
ll have paid for 32 and received 18 absolutely free!

267 HCK 4534
467 HCK 4535

me   (Please Print)

dress   Apt. #

y   State/Prov.   Zip/Postal Code

erms and prices subject to change without notice.
ales Tax applicable in N.Y. Canadian residents will be charged applicable provincial taxes
nd GST. All orders are subject to approval.
3AB01R   © 2000 Harlequin Enterprises Limited

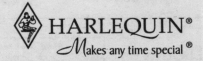

INDULGE IN A QUIET MOMENT
WITH HARLEQUIN

Get a FREE

Quiet Moments Bath Spa

with just two proofs of purchase from
ny of our four special collector's editions in May.

Harlequin® is sure to make your time special this Mother's Day
with four special collector's editions featuring a short story
PLUS a complete novel packaged together in one volume!

ollection #1   Intrigue abounds in a collection featuring *New York Times*
bestselling author Barbara Delinsky and Kelsey Roberts.

ollection #2   Relationships? Weddings? Children? = *New York Times*
bestselling author Debbie Macomber and Tara Taylor Quinn
at their best!

ollection #3   Escape to the past with *New York Times* bestselling author
Heather Graham and Gayle Wilson.

ollection #4   Go West! With *New York Times* bestselling author
Joan Johnston and Vicki Lewis Thompson!

Plus Special Consumer Campaign!
Each of these four collector's editions will feature a
"FREE QUIET MOMENTS BATH SPA" offer.
See inside book in May for details.

Only from
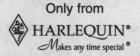
HARLEQUIN®
Makes any time special ®

Where the bond of family, tradition and honor run as deep and are as vast as the great Lone Star state, that's...

Texas families are at the heart of the next Harlequin 12-book continuity series.

HARLEQUIN®
INTRIGUE
is proud to launch this brand-new series of books by some of your very favorite authors.

Look for

SOMEONE'S BABY
by Dani Sinclair
On sale May 2001

SECRET BODYGUARD
by B.J. Daniels
On sale June 2001

UNCONDITIONAL SURRENDER
by Joanna Wayne
On sale July 2001

Available at your favorite retail outlet.

HARLEQUIN®
Makes any time special ®

Visit us at www.eHarlequin.com

HITT